T0008828

"We need to get

Shouts echoed down t

"Wait, there are more samples. I need to get them all," Kinsley replied.

"No, you don't," Brett insisted.

She ignored him and gathered the rest.

"There, I see a light," a male voice whispered.

Brett and Kinsley turned off their lights simultaneously. They'd given themselves away. He hoped it was worth it.

But there's no way we're making it out of here without light. "Let's go." He shone his flashlight and they moved deeper into the lava tubes.

Why had the men suddenly decided to come for them in the cave? Had they been waiting for Kinsley to finally come here?

"Look, Brett. There's light up ahead."

They turned off their flashlights and headlamps. "There's a hole in the ceiling. Can we get out through there?"

"Are you crazy? We should just keep going to the exit."

Except, someone could be waiting for them when they came out.

Elizabeth Goddard is the award-winning author of more than thirty novels and novellas. A 2011 Carol Award winner, she was a double finalist in the 2016 Daphne du Maurier Award for Excellence in Mystery/Suspense and a 2016 Carol Award finalist. Elizabeth graduated with a computer science degree and worked in high-level software sales before retiring to write full-time.

Visit the Author Profile page at LoveInspired.com for more titles.

DEADLY
SABOTAGE

ELIZABETH GODDARD

LOVE INSPIRED SUSPENSE
INSPIRATIONAL ROMANCE

LOVE INSPIRED® SUSPENSE

INSPIRATIONAL ROMANCE

Recycling programs
for this product may
not exist in your area.

ISBN-13: 978-1-335-59920-9

Deadly Sabotage

For questions and comments about the quality of this book, please contact us
at CustomerService@Harlequin.com.

Love Inspired
22 Adelaide St. West, 41st Floor
Toronto, Ontario M5H 4E3, Canada
www.LoveInspired.com

Printed in U.S.A.

To appoint unto them that mourn in Zion, to give unto them beauty for ashes, the oil of joy for mourning, the garment of praise for the spirit of heaviness; that they might be called trees of righteousness, the planting of the Lord, that he might be glorified.

—*Isaiah* 61:3

Dedicated to Jesus, my Lord and Savior
who turns ashes to beauty.

ONE

Tick tock. Tick tock. Tick tock.

Beneath her lab coat, a shiver crawled over her arms.

When the hum of the medical refrigerators cycled off, the wall clock's ticking filled the silence.

Kinsley Langell had been looking through the eyepiece of the microscope for too long. She sat up and rubbed her blurry eyes. She often worked late into the evening at the Stevens Lab, so should be used to it by now, but tonight she couldn't shake her sense of unease. The lab was partitioned off from their main offices—hers and Max's—by a glass wall, and she could look through the big window at dark offices. The dim lighting didn't chase away the shadows.

She'd never been afraid to work alone, so wasn't sure why she felt unsettled tonight.

Unable to shake the bad feeling, she hopped

off the stool and put the borosilicate glass slide away. Recorded her observations and then glanced at the clock. She should get out of there. Go home. Her boss, Max Stevens, always told her she worked too hard. But she *lived* for her work, for the chance to find new cures for deadly diseases like the one that killed her sister, Olivia. Still, the workday had to end at some point. She wouldn't be able to do her job well if she didn't get enough rest. Kinsley cleaned up her workstation, then started to pull off her lab coat.

Movement drew her attention to the glass wall. Max rushed down the hallway toward the lab. He'd already donned his white coat and hurriedly entered the code to allow him entrance. He looked different somehow. When he looked up, she realized his face was a mix of excitement and tension. He must have found something that energized him.

Her mood suddenly shifted, and the sense of unease disappeared. She smiled as the door opened with a whoosh, then closed tightly behind him.

"I wasn't expecting you back this week and certainly not tonight." She started pulling her lab coat back on all the way. Might as well stay if Max was here. "I thought you'd spend at least another day in the caves. You love those dark crawl spaces."

She'd only gone with him once to explore and gather samples. Max's lab specialized in drug discovery in caves, which provided a unique environment conducive to the production of all sorts of antimicrobials and anticancer compounds—from natural and organic sources, rather than synthetic. Only a few labs like Max's existed.

And he'd helped her to fulfill her dreams of finding a way to fight and treat emerging illnesses.

"I finished up early." He gathered his samples out of his kit, then placed them in cold storage.

Then he turned to her. His smile seemed forced at first but then grew genuine. "You know I have a one-track mind. While I'm always glad to see you, I thought you'd be gone by now."

"You know me, working late if I can. Since you weren't here to force me to quit, I worked a little later." She offered a sheepish grin. If he was here and had found something new and exciting, she wanted to be part of it.

"That's why you need me to tell you to go home and get a life."

Right. They both knew she poured everything into her job and took her work home with her when she could. He gently grabbed her shoulders and turned her around toward the door, then started to walk her forward.

"But you just got here," she said. "I can help. I want to hear all about the trip."

Max continued pushing. "In the morning, Kinsley. I promised your parents I'd look out for you, and I've done my best, but you need to cooperate."

"And I appreciate all you've done." He'd been there for her ever since her parents had been killed in an accident. But that did leave her with a question—one she'd always wondered but had never asked. Tonight, somehow, the moment seemed right. "Would you have hired me if you hadn't been Dad's best friend?"

"I hired you because you're fully qualified— what with a PhD. in chemical biology. The fact that you're my best friend's daughter didn't hurt." He winked, teasing her.

She shrugged out of his grip. "Okay. I'll leave if you give me something. Tell me just one thing about the trip."

"The cave was dark and slimy." He grinned.

"Oh, you." She gently punched his arm. "The cave is always dark and slimy." Part of the reason she'd only ever gone with him once. That, and well, he'd never invited her to go a second time.

"I won't learn anything until I get these specimens under the microscope. You know that."

She sighed. The process took so long. "At least this has paid off for us in the past." They already had two drugs going through the intensive testing and approval process via New-Bio Scientific, Inc., the big biopharma company with which they partnered to take the drugs the rest of the way to market.

"Yes. If only it didn't take years. And since it takes so long, going home earlier and having a life isn't going to kill you."

She gave an exaggerated roll of her eyes. Max was being more pushy than usual in trying to get her out of here. "I give up. I'll leave you alone. I think spending too much time in a cave is turning you into a recluse."

She removed her jacket and tossed the gloves. "I'll see you in the morning, Max. Promise me that you won't work too late."

"No promises, Kinsley."

As he pulled out the traps he created to catch microbes, he appeared giddy as a schoolboy. No surprise there—she knew this was his favorite part. Next, he would purify the microbes and get DNA. He had to know if they were distinct from known bacteria. That was the whole point of novelty drug discovery—finding *new* bacteria to explore in pharmaceutical uses.

"You sure you don't want me to stay behind? I can help you prep them for fermentation. Just sayin'…"

"Go home, Kinsley. Plenty to do tomorrow."

"You're the boss." Blowing out a frustrated breath, she waited for the door to open—it was specially designed to minimize contamination issues. The suction released, and the door opened, the familiar sound oddly comforting. Kinsley exited the lab and the door closed behind her.

In the darker hallway, the bright lights inside the sealed lab emphasized Max's expression, confirming that he'd found something unique.

Disappointment lodged in her gut that he didn't want her to be part of it, but she was being ridiculous. He needed this quiet time alone to focus, and he would share with her in the morning. She went to her office and grabbed her purse and jacket. She and Max worked well together, and so far, he hadn't hired any additional staff. Max outsourced for all other non-research staffing needs—like bookeeping and accounting. His lease agreement took care of the building and utilities. liked to keep it simple and small.

She stepped outside. Even in late April, the evenings could cool off in the Puget Sound region in western Washington. But she enjoyed the cool weather and the way the rain left the air smelling fresh and clean.

She entered the code to let herself out so the alarm system would remain armed, then stepped outside. Lush and thick foliage surrounded the small parking lot, and even the few security lights couldn't chase away all the shadows. Washington was referred to as the Evergreen State, and Seattle, Emerald City, for a reason. For once, she didn't appreciate the trees because they seemed to emphasize that sense of unease she'd felt earlier. It grew stronger as she made her way to her car parked in the dark beneath two large cedar trees.

She rummaged for her keys in her purse, wishing she'd gotten them out sooner.

A concussive force hit her in the back and shoved her forward, then slammed her into the shrubs, face-first. A loud explosion rocked the air around her, vibrating through her core. In a daze, she struggled to get her bearings.

What...happened?

Kinsley's heart pounded. She couldn't breathe as fear choked her.

Need. Air. I need air.

Finally, she sucked in a breath. Then another breath. Then finally, another, and this time she became aware of the acrid odor of ash, burning metal and chemicals filling the air. Fire crackled behind her and heated the cold night. Ferns had cushioned her fall, but she felt the sting of scratches and the pain of bruises. Suddenly, the world around her came into clear focus.

Feeling every ache in her body, she rolled over and watched the building ablaze. Her mind slowly wrapped around the incomprehensible. An explosion? What had Max done?

Realization dawned.

Max!

He was still inside the lab!

She had to help him. To save him.

A voice sounded close, but she couldn't place it. She tried to get up and call for help, but her body was too shaky to cooperate. A man spoke into his cell phone and walked next to another man near the building. Maybe they were calling for help. She needed to tell them she was here too, and they could help her.

Except her earlier unease returned. The men weren't acting frantic or concerned. Their reaction seemed strange. Still, she wasn't thinking clearly, and her odd, instinctual fear was likely unfounded. She started to get up again and stand on shaky legs. She even cried out, but her voice sounded feeble and weak against the blaze.

As the men walked past, their eyes on the fire, she heard one man's voice loud and clear.

"They're both dead. Don't worry. It'll look like an accident just like you wanted."

Kinsley froze. *What had he said?*

He must have put his cell on speaker so his partner could hear.

"Are you sure?" The voice sounded over the cell. "The police have ways of finding the truth."

Kinsley gasped to herself. She recognized the voice but couldn't remember to whom it belonged. Where had she heard his voice before?"

"Don't worry. I have a friend inside the local PD."

Brett Honor tugged his jacket tighter as the wind picked up. He loved to walk this beach at night, especially when the moon was full, and listen to the waves crashing into the rocky outcroppings and sea stacks along the shore. To his way of thinking, this was the most beautiful place on earth. Depending on the day, the Pacific Northwest weather could still be windy and cold, but he didn't mind. If the day was nice, he might lounge in a chair on the sandy shores, or if it was too rainy or windy, he would sleep or read in the rental house. Either way, the scenery brought him peace. It was why he'd chosen to stay in Washington only a couple of hours from West Ridge—the small town in the south-east part of Tacoma metropolitan area where the Honor Protection Specialists headquarters were located.

He was supposed to travel to the Caribbean or the Fiji Islands, like his older brother Ayden, who founded the bodyguard protection and investigations business, had suggested. Really, Ayden had demanded he take time off and head to a tropical island and relax on the beach.

Brett thought back to his words.

"You put on a great front for everyone, but I can tell you need a break. And you need help."

Ayden understood what it meant to live with past trauma, and Brett thought he'd put what happened behind him. But when his helicopter crashed recently during an operation to protect a client, the nightmares had come back. As the months passed, he'd tried to hide his issues but instead of getting better, he was getting worse. And Ayden saw right through him. Hence the enforced vacation. But while his brother could force him to take the time off, he couldn't dictate where Brett went. This was where he wanted to be—not on some tropical beach.

The wind blew hard and buffeted his body as he walked right into it. Weirdly, tonight, he enjoyed what felt like a cold slap in the face, and pinpricks against his cheek. What he didn't enjoy was the fact that his cell phone continued to buzz. He'd been ignoring that buzz and should reach into his pocket to silence it, but he was afraid to touch it. Looking at it at all would mean he'd see who was trying to reach him and then he'd want to answer.

He should have left the cell in the bungalow he'd rented for this stay. It was probably one of his brothers or his sister checking on him. He had only his siblings in his life now, so who else could it be?

Okay. I'm here. Taking a break. So give me a break.

Finally, he had no choice if he wanted any peace but to fish the cell from his pocket to silence it completely. Unfortunately, just like he thought, he looked at the number. He planned to ignore the call if it was from his family.

But it wasn't from Ayden, Caine, or Everly. Instead, his heart pounded. He recognized the number from long ago. It must be a mistake. Or a weird coincidence.

Curious, he glanced at the text that had come in from that same number.

Kinsley Langell?

He stumbled on a rock and caught himself. Weird that he remembered her number. Stranger that he was seeing it now.

Why would Kinsley Langell be trying to reach me? He'd broken things off with her three years ago. Hurt them both, he was sure. No way would she call him unless she was desperate.

He had a new number, though, so how had she gotten his number?

Should he respond? Like he needed more heartache. He couldn't go through that again.

But if she was calling, she must need help. He returned the call and she immediately answered. "Brett? Brett Honor?"

At the sound of her voice, a knot lodged in his throat. *Kinsley...*

A few breaths passed before he could even respond. "The same. Kinsley, I'm surprised to hear from you." Could he sound less stunned?

"Brett, I need your help. I didn't know who else to call."

Really? She could think of no one else? He never thought he'd hear from her again. He didn't *want* to hear from her again because it reminded him of those dark times in the hospital, and the crash. And if anyone had asked him yesterday, he'd have said that she would never want to hear from him either. Whatever was going on, it must be bad. He frowned and turned to walk back to the bungalow.

"You must be desperate to call me."

"I *am*."

"What's going on?"

"I died tonight."

He stopped in his tracks. Scratched his head. Oh, no. "Are you…are you self-medicating?" As in using drugs?

"What? Of course not. What I mean is someone tried to kill me, and they *think* I'm dead. I need to *stay* dead on the official record and… I need your help to live. To survive this. Please. I have no one else, and I know you have skills. I can't trust anyone else."

That made a little more sense but was still confusing as well as terrifying.

This was serious. He headed toward his bungalow as he talked. He couldn't turn her down. "Who tried to kill you? What happened? Did you call the police?"

"I can't call the police—I think they might be involved. I can't explain it all now. At last not on the phone, Brett. It's complicated. But I'll tell you everything when I see you."

Right. She was right. He wanted answers but now wasn't the time. Her safety was a priority. She'd gotten his number somehow, and since she was calling, probably knew he was in Washington. "Where are you?"

"You'll have to meet me. I don't have a car, and I need to ditch my cell phone. I'm hiding and I'm scared."

"Okay, where? Just tell me where?" *Please let it be close.*

"I'm in a homeless camp. I'll be walking around. I'll look for you—what will you be driving?"

"Kinsley, be careful." Someone had just tried to kill her.

"It's the best place to hide, okay? But hurry or someone might start asking questions. I need to disappear."

"I need the address."

"I'll be in the camp near Oak Avenue and I-5 north of Olympia."

He was curious about how she'd found his number and how she knew that he was even in Washington. But he could ask her that later.

He looked the location up on a digital map and found it. Oh, boy. "I'm going to park at the Texaco gas station near that intersection."

"When, Brett? I..." She choked back a sob.

"As fast as I can. It'll take me at most a couple of hours. Three tops. I'm on the coast today. Now, I hate to have you do this, because it's our only link, but you're right—you need to toss your phone. How...how did you get my number?" Why did he need to know that now?

"I—" The connection suddenly went dead.

"Kinsley? Kinsley?" He shouted into his cell and drew a look from a couple exiting a rental house as he approached his. He should call his siblings, but Ayden wouldn't want him on this because he was supposed to be taking a break, so Ayden would then take it over himself. But no way would Brett let anyone else handle this. Kinsley had sought him out, so he would be there for her. That is, if he could find her before she disappeared forever.

TWO

Of course her phone had died so she couldn't call him back if she wanted to.

Or needed to. She'd just have to hold out until he got here. What else was she going to do? In the meantime, she had to destroy the SIM card anyway, because her cell could still give off signals that would allow her to be located if someone had access to the right kind of software. Something she'd learned from the movies, since she spent a lot of time watching them alone in the evenings, even when she got home late.

Kinsley tugged out the SIM card, which was difficult without drawing attention. She smashed it, then discarded the cell in a puddle before finally taking a moment to really look around her. A fire burned in an old rusty can. Various-sized tents had been set up around the camp in the dense woods between the road and the freeway. Some relatively complex dwell-

ings—multiple tents and boxes—had been cob-
bled together beneath the freeway as well.

I need someplace safe to wait. An incredulous laugh bubbled up, but she stifled it so she
wouldn't draw attention.

She wasn't sure she could stay in this spot,
with cars and trucks speeding along the highway so close. It felt too exposed.

Feeling both terrified and numb all over, she
found a small, more sheltered corner to sit in
the shadows and keep warm, if she could, for
the next couple of hours. She would often drive
right by this homeless camp and would hand
out bags filled with essential items she'd created. Protein bars, toothbrushes and toothpaste,
and other daily essentials people often took for
granted.

Unless they were homeless.

It was all she could do.

Unfortunately, she also smelled the scent of
marijuana and knew that other drugs were likely
being used as well, and that made her uncomfortable and wary. She hoped that as long as she
remained unnoticed, she'd be fine.

No. That wasn't true. She wouldn't be fine
ever again.

What had just happened back there? Every
time she closed her eyes, she felt the blast shove
her to the ground. Heard the boom and the

flames crackle. Then those voices and their incriminating words.

Max... I can't believe you're gone.

He was all she had left.

Hot tears gushed out the corners of her eyes. She wiped them away. Not here. Not now. Her goal had been to blend in and stay hidden, and, as she made her way from the blast zone, moving from shadow to shadow to get as far away as she could, she'd ended up in the homeless camp. People had mostly settled into their tents for the evening, and no one had really noticed her yet, for which she was grateful.

In the shadows of a large cedar tree trunk, she felt somewhat protected from the light rain that started to fall. She closed her eyes. The images started up and so did the tears. This time she couldn't stop them from burning down her cheeks. Not good. She didn't want to draw attention by outright sobbing.

Just hold it together for a little longer. Brett will be here soon.

Max, oh, Max.

But she could grieve later, once she got to safety.

For now, she tried to hold herself together by thinking through the sequence of events—what had happened, and what *needed* to happen now to keep her safe. She thought about the complete destruction of the lab—a fire had continued to rage even as she'd snuck away. The two men had remained in the shadows as others gathered to watch. She couldn't be seen alive by them, or by the police, considering one of them said he'd had inside connections.

She could identify the men responsible, so they had every reason to want her dead.

Nausea swept through her.

Max was dead. Dad's best friend who'd become kind of a father figure for her too. The shock of his death along with the blast rocked through her despite her attempts to redirect her thoughts, and more nausea hit her.

Did she have a concussion? She probably needed a doctor to look her over. Her parents had been doctors, and she was a microbiologist so knew anatomy and physiology in general terms. The blast could have caused damage to her internal organs, but there was nothing she could do about that at the moment. She also knew that she had precious little time before the killers discovered she was still alive. She wanted to use that time wisely.

Still…

What was I thinking?

Brett Honor?

Really?

He'd been the first person she had thought

to call. *Why?* She hadn't spoken to him in so long. He probably had a wife or a girlfriend. He had a life.

But with everyone in *her* life now dead, she had no one else to turn to. She couldn't trust the police until she knew who those men were and to whom they were connected in the PD. No one was going to believe her without the evidence, and she needed to learn more before she could come forward or she would just be the prover-bial sitting duck.

She wasn't stupid enough to think she could do this on her own.

Brett had been in the military, and after he had broken things off without explanation, she'd kept up with what little news she was able to find on him. He had gone into the Coast Guard and had been in the States for a while, and then went to work at Honor Protection Specialists with his siblings in Washington. And during a moment of loneliness a few months ago, she'd done some digging and found his number on a busness website. She'd been furious at herself then and was grateful she had the good sense to not make that call. But she was glad she'd had the number tonight.

God, please, please help me. I don't under-stand what's going on, but I'm so scared. You are always with me, so be with me now.

Because other than God, she was utterly alone.

Well, except for Brett—but he wasn't really in her life. He'd been her hero once before, so maybe that's why she had never forgotten him, and her desperate, scared mind had thought of him in this moment.

Closing her eyes, she let herself think back to the past. Her parents had worked with Doctors Without Borders, and she had gone on an assignment with them one summer between college semesters. Severe flooding had struck in Bangladesh, where they had been working, and she and her family had needed rescuing. The US Military had been there for them, and she'd quickly fallen for the helicopter pilot, Brett Honor. He'd been caring and gentle, and his smile and eyes had captured her heart that day.

They'd kept in touch. During her college breaks or his military leave, they were together. She had even imagined that he was the one, but he broke things off with her without explanation. Left her with a broken heart. Okay, maybe she shouldn't have thought back to that time. Now she wished she hadn't called him. Embarrassment flooded her.

Stop. Just stop it.

She was a professional and a levelheaded person. After the breakup she'd become laser focused on her job and finding and developing new drugs. She couldn't have done that had she been with Brett, so in the end it all worked out for the best. She had no emotional ties to him now, and he was simply the means to an end.

A glance at her watch told her she was already late to meet Brett at the gas station. How had she let that happen?

Heart pounding, Brett was starting to get worried about Kinsley. She hadn't shown up at their meeting place. Maybe he should make his way to the homeless camp to see if he could find her. Then he saw her crossing the freeway, looking haggard and terrified. His heart jumped to his throat, and he ran to the edge of the parking lot to meet her and grab her up in his arms. "Kinsley, I was so worried."

She held on to him as if she was holding on to her life, then stepped away. At her disheveled appearance, pain ignited in his heart. Anger burst through him and a fierce protectiveness rose up.

She started to cry and his heart ached. He wanted to cry with her. "You're okay now. You're okay…"

Stepping back, she wiped her nose and swiped at her cheeks. Rubbed her eyes. "Let's get out of here."

He nodded. *That-a-girl*. Taking her hand, he

got her settled in his truck and started up the engine.

He thought to talk it over. See if she was okay, though he knew she couldn't possibly be okay after what she'd been through tonight.

"Go, just go. Get me out of here."

He steered out of the parking lot and onto the freeway. "You need medical attention, Kinsley. I'm no doctor, but you look injured."

"No hospital. No authorities."

She might be out of her head. *What to do. What to do.*

"I'm going to need to know why not."

"I don't know who I can trust, okay?" As Kinsley shared her story his gut twisted into an impossible knot.

"And the voice I heard... I recognized it. I don't know how, but I just did. Like it belongs to an important person. Someone who knows me or Max. I'm afraid to go to the police without knowing who is trying to kill me. Since one of the saboteurs is connected to someone inside the PD, they could show up somewhere and take me out there." Brett weaved in and out of traffic. The good news was that she seemed clearheaded and rational. The bad news was that from the sound of things, she had very good reason to be afraid. A hospital or police station wasn't an option. "I have an idea. My parents had a good friend who took care of their horses for years. He's a veterinarian."

"A vet? You want to take me to a vet?"

"You got a better idea?"

She plopped her head back against the seat. "No. And right now, all I want to do is curl up in a ball in a nice comfy bed and wake up to realize this was all just a bad dream. A nightmare."

Me too. "I'm so sorry this happened, Kinsley. But I'm here to help you. We'll get through this together, okay?" He looked to the side to catch her eye, wanting to see if his words had brought her any comfort.

But she'd already fallen asleep. She must have been exhausted and then adrenaline had crashed, and since she trusted Brett, she was able to let go and let sleep take her. Anger built in his gut that she'd gone through some horrific trauma. And amazement that she'd called *him* of all people.

Almost being murdered was a worst-case scenario so she was definitely desperate, but he still couldn't wrap his mind around the fact she had called him. He might bring in his siblings at Honor Protection Specialists, depending on what he found out. A half hour into the drive, he steered off the freeway and onto a state highway that he followed for another twenty miles or so, and then, finally, a rural road. He sure hoped that Vince Hefflinger was still around and still practicing medicine. He didn't have the number in his new phone so he couldn't call to check. He'd just have to hope for the best.

Kinsley suddenly startled awake. She screamed and thrashed.

Surprised, he swerved, and then pulled onto the shoulder. After parking, he shifted toward her and gently gripped her arms. "Kinsley you're okay. You're okay. It's me Brett. You're with me."

She gasped and kept sucking in air. "Oh, Brett. I'm sorry. I'm so sorry."

She was hyperventilating.

"Just calm down and breathe."

He exaggerated his slow breathing and modeled it for her until finally she was breathing like someone who wasn't scared out of her mind. Then he released her and fully shifted back to his seat.

Her eyes flashed to him, then down, as though she was embarrassed. "Sorry, I'm not usually so out of control."

"You've been through a lot. It's understandable."

She finally lifted her face and stared at the darkness outside of the windows. "Where are we?"

"We're almost to the vet's place." He dug

around in the back seat and found a bottle of water, wishing that he had thought of it sooner. "Here, drink this. You're probably thirsty."

She guzzled the water, then rested her head and closed her eyes. "I thought things might look a little better after I got some rest. But they don't. Just...help me figure this out, please."

"I will. But maybe we'd be better off bringing some more people into this. My siblings—"

"Just you, Brett. No one else. Please."

"You know it's only a matter of time before the news is out that only one body was recovered, and then after a time, *whose* body was recovered. Then they'll know you're still alive. The situation might end up going sideways in a hurry."

"I know. But that just means we need to act fast—find a way to figure out who's behind this while they think I'm dead. I just don't know what."

"We'll do what we can. What do you know about their plan?"

"They said it would look like an accident. I'm the only person who knows that it wasn't. I can also identify the two men responsible for the explosion. I don't know them, but I saw their faces briefly. It was dark out even with security lighting and the building ablaze, but I still think I could identify them."

"Regarding this being intentional rather than an accident, don't discount law enforcement forensics. They might discover the truth on their own. Maybe they'll even figure out that one of their own is in on it. But with or without that knowledge, they will learn this wasn't an accident."

He pulled up the drive and parked in front of a well-kept farmhouse with blue-gray siding and a white wraparound porch. "Look, we're here."

The porch light came on. Motion detectors?

"Wait here." He stepped out of the vehicle, hiked to the porch and bounded up the few steps, stopping on the top step the moment the front door opened.

A fifty-something woman stood in the door aiming a double-barreled shotgun at him.

THREE

What is going on?

Kinsley covered her mouth.

She wanted to scream. A woman stepped out of her house and pointed a long gun at Brett. *What more could happen on this the worst day of her life?* Not counting her parents' death, or her sister's, of course!

God, I can't take anymore.

Kinsley had no idea what she could do to help. She eyed the ignition—and the keys were still in it. At least she could escape if she had to, but then again, leaving Brett wasn't an option. The woman lowered the gun.

Brett must have done some fast talking. But it was obvious the person hadn't recognized him. Maybe Brett had expected a different welcome. He continued talking to the woman in an animated way, moving his arms around a lot, then he gestured to the vehicle where Kinsley sat while he spoke.

Coming to a stranger for help, a vet, no less, might have been a mistake. Still, he was right. Kinsley needed someone with medical experience to examine her. She physically hurt all over. And well, mentally, psychologically she hurt too but she could wait to get help in that regard if she needed it.

But having another opinion besides her own—even from a veterinarian—would reassure her regarding her physical injuries, so she could focus on learning why someone had killed Max and *tried* to kill her. Why had someone destroyed the Stevens Lab?

That Max was dead, the lab destroyed—all of it intentional—seemed surreal.

Brett and the gray-haired woman stepped off the porch and trudged toward Kinsley. She wished she could slide down into the floorboard and disappear. At the passenger side, Brett opened the door and crouched. He took her hand.

So gentle. So caring. It reminded her of his brave helicopter rescue and the reason she'd fallen for him to begin with.

And here he was again, still so kind and gentle as if she was a frightened animal he was trying not to spook. Kinsley was no coward, and she wasn't usually this fragile. Or scared.

I need to snap out of this.

"Kinsley," Brett said, "this is Dr. Hefflinger's daughter, Camille. She took over his veterinarian business several years ago when he passed on. She's willing to help you. I know she's a stranger to you, but I believe we can trust her. My family has known the Hefflingers for years. Camille hasn't seen me in a couple of decades and just didn't recognize me at the door. There's been a sharp increase in crime in the area lately and she wasn't taking any chances."

"Hence the shotgun." Kinsle sighed. "I don't know, Brett. Maybe this isn't such a good idea."

Camille leaned in. "You don't know me, but I've been through a few bad experiences in my life. I was grateful that someone stepped in to help when I needed it. God is with you, Kinsley. I was supposed to go out of town tonight, but I had a feeling—I don't know what, exactly, other than I thought I should stay home tonight. Now you're here. I believe God is looking out for you. Will you come in and let me have a look at you?"

A feeling of calm settled over her, and Kinsley let her guard down. She sensed she could trust Camille, after all, and finally nodded. Brett gave her a tenuous smile, then offered his hand. She took it and he helped her out of the vehicle. After sitting, she had stiffened up like she had a severe case of rheumatoid arthritis. Camille stepped on the other side of her and helped Brett assist Kinsley up the porch steps into her home. A fire was going in the fireplace. tThe room was cozy and warm and welcoming and the scent of both woodsmoke and vanilla filled the air.

They guided her into a bedroom, and Camille gestured for Kinsley to sit on the bed covered in what looked like a hand-sewn quilt in burnt orange and purple. Beautiful and comforting.

Then it hit her. "Wait. You're not taking me to your clinic?"

Camille's chuckle was a pleasant and comforting sound. "My clinic is up the road. But even so, I think you'd be more comfortable here. It's not exactly designed to accommodate human patients. If Brett will give us some privacy, I'll give you an exam to the best of my ability."

Brett held her gaze, waiting for her answer.

"I'm good, Brett, thank you. You can go, but—" she gave him a timid grin "—not too far."

The smallest of smiles lifted the right side of his lips, as if he was glad that she wanted him to stay, but sad about the reasons. And she was reading far too much into that look. If only she didn't know him so well that she could read and understand every single look. If only being with him didn't remind her of the good times they had together.

And the bad.

After holding her gaze longer than necessary, he nodded, then exited the room and shut the door.

Camille turned to Kinsley. "Can you tell me what happened? It would help inform my exam."

Kinsley hung her head. She didn't want to involve one more person in the danger.

"You don't have to give me the details, but what happened to you? Were you in a car wreck?"

If only. "Nothing like that. It was an explosion. I was walking to my car when the building behind me exploded. It felt like it kicked me to the ground. Like someone punched me in the back. I was forced to the ground into some ferns, thankfully. I might feel even more bruised if I'd hit the asphalt instead."

"Did you lose consciousness?"

Kinsley shook her head. "I don't think so. No."

Camille released a breath, and her shoulders dropped as if she was relieved. "Good."

She opened a drawer and pulled out a stethoscope. "Fortunately for you, I keep medical instruments close. You never know when someone is going to need help. She listened to Kinsley's heart and her lungs. Felt around her abdomen and asked if anything hurt.

"Everything hurts."

Camille frowned. "It's understandable that you would feel bruised after what you just described."

After putting her stethoscope away, she examined Kinsley's head. "I need to clean a cut at your temple. Other than being banged up, you appear to be in good health, but I can't know for certain that you don't have traumatic injuries to your organs, or even your brain. Brett explained that you're in danger and need to stay under the radar, but I advise you to try to see a physician as quickly as possible so appropriate tests can be done. Pay attention to any symptoms. If you start experiencing dizziness or extreme thirst, then I advise you to go to the ER."

Kinsley knew all this, but still, it helped that Camille had taken the time to look her over and confirm she wasn't going to die.

At least not yet.

But if the men after her managed to catch up with her, her days could be few.

By the time that Brett parked near the bungalow rental on the beach with Kinsley in the passenger seat, it was close to three in the morning. He hadn't been sure bringing her back here was the best idea. Camille had been kind enough to offer to let them sleep at her home for the night. But he'd already asked enough of her as it was, and didn't want to bring danger to her door. She'd given Brett the basics—Kinsley appeared to be okay but without tests and perhaps an MRI, Kinsley's condition couldn't be fully evaluated. He could have guessed that, but he had hoped for a better answer.

Am I making the wrong move in not taking her straight to the hospital? Even if I did, she could simply refuse treatment.

Why were some decisions so insanely hard? He could be taking her to her death—ironically—by taking her to a hospital. That, and well, she claimed that she would disappear, and he wouldn't see her again if he tried. He'd lost her trust once before—on matters of the heart, at least—and he couldn't bring himself to do more damage to her faith in him than had already been done.

Clearly, she needed help. He couldn't let her continue this spiral into danger alone. Nope. He would spiral right along with her. Really, he would try to pull her out before she lost her life the next time. If Brett had his way, there wouldn't be a next time.

She finally stirred and looked at him with her amazing blue-green eyes. Thanks to Camille, she had a bandage at her temple now and her face was free from dark smudges. Her thick brunette hair had been in tangles when he'd found her at a homeless camp, but she'd obviously run a brush through it at Camille's.

Though a few years older, she remained as beautiful as he remembered but it was the tender warmth in her eyes that still took his breath way.

He swallowed past the lump in his throat. "We're here."

She glanced around. "Where is here? There's nothing to see really, except for darkness."

Clouds had gathered, hiding the moon, and the town was too far to reflect light against them.

"A bungalow I rented. This is where I was when you called. No one knows I'm here."

He opened the door first and the inside light came on casting shadows.

Kinsley squinted her eyes. "I…you're sure it's safe?"

"Safest place I know for now." And he doubted anyone would think to look for him to find her.

At least…at first.

She got out. After grabbing the bag holding the two burner phones he'd bought at an all-night convenience store, he rushed around to help her. She stood tall but looked stiff and in pain.

Kinsley lifted a hand to hold him off. "I'm okay. I'm good. I'm just sore. Camille gave me some pain relievers. I just need to sleep." She shut the door and angled her head. "I hear the ocean. Smell it too."

"I hope that's okay."

"It's nice. And Brett... I can't thank you enough."

"No need to thank me." Though she'd refused his help at first, she ended up letting him assist her up the steps of the porch and into the small quaint vacation rental on the beach.

If he had been in Fiji, he couldn't have helped her. Maybe Camille was right, and God had been looking out for Kinsley tonight. He didn't know about her friend Max though. These kinds of questions of the universe were above his pay grade. As he flipped on lights and pulled shades for privacy, he thought that protecting Kinsley might also be above his pay grade, given that she was his former girlfriend. Except she wasn't contracted through protection services, so he wasn't getting paid.

It was Kinsley—he didn't want to be paid. She was his own personal and private assignment.

"The bungalow has two rooms," he said. "It was what they had. Nobody has been here with me. Let me show you to the extra room. I'm here, Kinsley. I'm here to protect you and help you. So just relax. Try to get some sleep tonight. We'll talk tomorrow."

He showed her into the room with the perfectly made bed and clean sheets. A bathroom prestocked by the rental company with toothpaste and disposable toothbrushes. Generic soap and shampoo.

At her raised eyebrows he shrugged. What could he say? He'd asked for a full-service rental. He didn't want to have to remember everything he might need.

She exited the bathroom, then whirled around. "I'll need some clothes, Brett. Unless, this vacation rental supplied those, too."

He chuckled, though this was hardly the time. "No. The closet is empty. Sorry. But I have some sweats and a T-shirt you can wear tonight. I'll pick something up for you in town tomorrow. Sleep in and I'll shop. Oh, I almost forgot." He tugged the box containing the burner cell out and tossed it on the bed. "Make sure to give me the number when you set it up. What else can I get you while I'm in town?"

"Hair dye and glasses. Scissors. I need to change my look. At some point, like you said, they'll know I didn't die and they'll be searching for me."

She was really going this far with it. And...

I guess I am too. "All right. I'll see you in the morning."

Without thinking he leaned in as if to kiss her. But stopped himself. Still, he was too close. So he spoke in a soft voice. "I...uh... I've got this, Kinsley. I've got you. I hope you know that." Despite that he'd broken her heart years ago.

"I know that about you, Brett. You're a good man when push comes to shove."

Push comes to shove? His dad used to say that too. It was an old phrase. Feelings of nostalgia rushed through him for all that he'd lost. He cleared his throat. "I'll be right back with those clothes."

She disappeared into the bathroom.

In his bedroom, he dug through his duffel and pulled out the clean clothes. Smelled them. They were still fresh enough.

Clothes handed off, Brett stood in the kitchen and drank a glass of water. So much had happened so fast, he hadn't had a chance to take a good long breath and think about what he was getting into. But really, what was there to think about?

Kinsley needed him. He wouldn't turn her down. End of story.

On his cell, he searched for news stories about what had happened, but he couldn't find what he needed.

Keeping the volume low, he turned on the television to see if any kind of breaking news would show up and let him know what the media or police thought of the incident. He could go through the HPS channels and learn more if needed and probably would eventually. That time would come, he had no doubt.

Kinsley said the man who spoke into the phone thought she and Max were dead—just like someone had wanted. So this had been a hit job. The voice on the other end of the cell had sounded familiar to her. Even more terrifying. Someone "close to home" wanted her dead.

Why a hit? Why her? Just because of her proximity to Max Stevens?

When a person got lost, there was an order of things to do to survive. Shelter always came first. Getting out of the harsh environment was a priority. Then water. Sending an SOS, finding help was important too.

Tonight, she had shelter.

He stopped on a news story regarding a lab that had exploded and had killed one person.

One person.

The anchorwoman said that authorities were looking into the cause, then she moved to a new story.

One person.

The big question now was if they had determined the identity of the one person who had died. Whoever had set the bomb off would likely be watching Max's house tonight as well as Kinsley's. She'd made the right call to pretend she was dead, not returning to her home or using any cards or getting cash at an ATM, and she'd left her car there at the lab. The authorities had to know that already and would be piecing things together.

He had to get some rest if he was going to be any help. After making sure the doors and windows were locked, he slept on the couch, just in case someone discovered he was helping Kinsley and also figured out where he was staying.

He needed to be ready to respond and kept his handgun within reach.

The chances were miniscule.

Just like the chances he would ever hear from her again.

Miniscule.

The next morning, he woke before sunrise. He wanted to knock on her door to check on her, but then again he didn't want to wake her. He left her a note on the counter letting her know that he'd gone to the store for a few items. Before he left, he flipped on the television again to see if he could learn anything more. Unfortunately, he learned something.

"Oh, no." Kinsley spoke from behind.

The anchorman's voice filled the room. "This morning, authorities are looking for Kinsley Langell for questioning in the explosion that killed Max Stevens."

FOUR

"Oh, no, Brett."

He quickly shut the television off. She covered her mouth and stepped forward, watching the news story and her face disappear from the screen. "It never even occurred to me—but of course they'd try to blame this on me. I don't know why I'm so shocked."

Brett rushed forward and gently took her arm. He ushered her to the sofa and urged her to sit as if she was a china doll. It seemed reasonable, considering at this moment she very much felt like she would break.

"Maybe I should have gone to the local police first and just taken that risk. Told them what I overheard—that someone within their ranks was connected. Maybe—"

"Shh. Kinsley, it's all right. I think you did the right thing. The only thing you could do. I would have done the same thing. You need to know more before you come forward with the truth. You need to know telling the truth won't get you killed."

She closed her eyes and took a deep breath.

I have to get my act together and be strong if I'm going to make it through this.

What did someone in a situation like this do? How often did this happen?

"Are you going to be okay? I was just about to head out to get your disguise, and I see now you're going to need it if you leave here even once."

"At least until I can identify the men who were there last night. Who the man behind the explosion is. I have no idea where to start looking." Well, that wasn't completely true. The lab and all the work Max did was a start.

"Let me make you breakfast. I want you to eat and relax and I'll be back soon. Then we'll brainstorm. You'll need to be rested and get your energy for a long day and the next phase of this."

A long day that could stretch into many days.

The next phase? Her shoulders sagged. "Okay. But I can make my own breakfast. You get the disguise and I promise that I'll eat and rest—if I can, though it's not likely—and I'll wait for you to get back. Then we can hash through this some more.

"Promise you won't even answer the door. Deadbolt it after I leave."

"I promise. Except, if it's you, I'll answer."

"How will you know it's me?"

She thought about it and glanced at the window.

"See? I don't even want you to look out the window. I'll call out, if it's me, if I need help. You'll recognize my voice, I hope." He grinned. "But stay away from the windows and don't open the door. My neighbor might come over and ask to borrow an egg."

"Really? People do that in vacation rentals?"

"Well, this one does. She asked to borrow an onion my first night here. I think she just wanted to be nosy. I hadn't gone shopping for groceries and even if I had, it would probably have been frozen dinners. Nothing I have to cook except for eggs for an omelet in the morning.

"Really? That's kind of sad."

He gave her the strangest smile, then Brett left her on the sofa and went to his room. She had to muster the energy to move off the sofa and head to the kitchen to make her breakfast, but it was so hard. She still ached all over and felt utterly drained. But Brett was right, food would help her feel better.

When Brett returned, he held a handgun.

"This is my Ruger LCP 2. Lightweight and compact. Perfect for you. Do you remember how to use a gun?"

She smiled. "The last time I held a gun was when you took me to the shooting range. That's been a while."

"That long?" He scratched his chin. "That's not good. But I don't feel right about leaving you here without a gun. It'll come back to you."

She wished she hadn't brought up that Brett had taken her to the shooting range on occasion back when they were together. Maybe that's why she'd thought of him first in the middle of her crisis.

She pushed from the sofa and approached to take the gun. "I think I remember, but it's been years, Brett."

He didn't hand it over just yet, but instead gave her a quick review and then set it on the side table.

"I hope I don't have to use it," she said.

"I hope you don't either, but better to have the option."

"What about you? Don't you need a gun?"

"I have my 9 mm." He stepped closer and his smoky gray eyes were intense and filled with concern. "I'm glad you called me, Kinsley."

With those words, he grabbed a jacket and exited the bungalow, leaving her standing there to watch him go. Through the window she wasn't supposed to look out, she watched him don the jacket over the T-shirt he wore that emphasized his sturdy chest and broad shoulders and ripped abs. She'd never cared about the fact he looked amazing—it was more that he was so kind and gentle and caring. That's why she'd been completely shocked when he'd broken off with her without an explanation.

And now he'd left her with the words *I'm glad you called me.*

What did he mean by that?

She moved to the kitchen and found eggs in the fridge. Did he mean… "I'm glad you called me because I protect people and you're clearly in need of protection"? or "I'm glad you called me, Kinsley, because I wanted to see you again"? Or did he mean, "I'm glad you called me, Kinsley, because I wanted to be the one to help you"? Or had he meant none of that?

Whatever he meant, if the meaning had been more personal, she couldn't let herself get caught up with Brett Honor—she wouldn't let herself be so completely broken ever again.

Love was a dangerous virus to which she had no intention of letting her heart be exposed.

For once Brett could appreciate the thick marine fog rolling off the Pacific as he took the lonely highway from the rental house into the nearest town, which was a good twenty minutes south. This part of the coast wasn't very populated—and that's how he liked it—away from civilization. But he'd picked the wrong place if he wanted his privacy. The vacation rentals were situated too close to each other; proven by his nosy neighbor.

But next time he'd know better. Next time?

He needed to focus on the real issues in front of him. Kinsley was here in his life again, though briefly. And *her* life was in danger. After he learned everything he could about what had happened, he needed to dig deep while protecting her.

One thing at a time, Brett. She needed a disguise.

Why hadn't he gotten more information about her actual size before he agreed to get her new clothes and a disguise. After the twenty-minute drive—wind and fog buffeting the vehicle—he finally steered into Nash, the nearest town that had a big box store and was more than just a lodge or trading post on the reservation.

After parking, he kept his head down and didn't make any eye contact while still trying to act normal and not like a guy who had anything to hide. He moved to the women's section and tried to focus on what size he thought she was.

He pulled jeans off the rack and eyed them and a size seven seemed right. Then he found some medium-sized T-shirts—probably too big, but that would give her more disguise options.

Then in the pharmacy department he found the hair color aisle. His head was spinning by the time he moved from one end to the other. But he had to make a decision and pushed the cart back to the middle.

He scratched his jaw at the choices. How did women decide? What color would Kinsley want? Why hadn't they discussed it? He could text her, but that would take more time. Since she had beautiful auburn hair, he would go dark brown. Then he searched for scissors. Over in the jewelry department he asked the clerk behind the counter where he could find fake glasses.

She briefly glanced at the basket and spotted the hair dye and women's clothing. She frowned slightly before her smile, then she pointed toward the sunglasses. "Maybe over there."

He was aware she watched him as he pushed the buggy around the corner. She probably thought he was creating his own disguise and she might remember him, when he didn't want to be remembered. *Good job, Brett.*

After purchasing everything he could think of to help Kinsley change her look, he paid for the items, pushed the squeaky cart out to his vehicle and tossed the sacks in the car.

When he finally got into his Toyota Highlander, he released a heavy sigh. Steering his vehicle out of the parking lot, he glanced in his mirrors, then stiffened. He'd seen that blue Subaru behind him earlier when he'd been driving around searching for the best place to shop. Was it coincidence? He'd better make sure he wasn't being followed before heading back out to the rental house on the beach.

The chances were *minuscule* that he'd already been discovered helping Kinsley.

There was that word again. *Miniscule.* For some reason, statistics weren't working when it came to Kinsley, and Brett would take no chances. He turned down a side road, then drove around the block and kept driving until he could park at the local gift shop in the small wind-blown downtown.

Wait and see.

He hoped he was overreacting. Realistically, there was no way anyone could possibly tie him to Kinsley—at least not yet. Their investigation into her life couldn't have made that much progress. He was an old boyfriend who had known her while he lived overseas.

He waited in the Highlander until he spotted

the Subaru pass slowly, then, unfortunately, the man parked one block down from him.

"Are you kidding me?" He wanted to confront the guy and get this over with. But that was just his frustration getting the best of him.

Brett waited in his vehicle to see what the Subaru driver would do. He couldn't exactly see him through the other parked cars, but he would be able to see if he exited his vehicle. The man got out of the Subaru and then moved to look in the window of a pet store. His actions didn't mean he wasn't following Brett. He'd remain watchful.

A text came through from Kinsley. He glanced at it.

Someone's at the door!

He replied.

Do not answer.

Brett growled. He'd already told her to stay away from the door and the windows. He didn't bother taking time to text her and ask whether the person at the door was knocking or trying to break in or were they simply standing there.

He quickly backed from the parking space, did an illegal U-turn in the middle of Main

Street, then drove the opposite direction. If the man tried to follow, he wouldn't be able to keep up with Brett.

He hadn't gotten the license plate number when he drove past. A woman walked behind the vehicle at that exact moment. Of course.

Lord, I hope I was wrong and that he wasn't following me.

Now he just had to get back to the house to make sure that Kinsley was okay. He drove like a maniac down the two-lane road but had to slow when the fog grew heavy.

Brett called Kinsley, but she didn't answer so he increased speed, even through the fog.

In the rearview mirror… No! *It can't be.*

He struggled to understand how he was being followed. Unless someone was watching her last night and followed him here this morning, he couldn't have been followed. But…how? Maybe someone had followed him but lost him in town last night so was waiting today.

It doesn't make sense.

Brett turned off the road and steered into the forest. The Subaru didn't follow. He tried calling Kinsley as he pulled back out on the main coastal road, then drove as fast as he could, watching for that stupid Subaru. Finally—after making sure no one was in sight—he steered onto the turnoff for the vacation rentals overlooking the ocean, then parked down from his bungalow. Leaving the sacks in the car for now, Brett hurried along the path and then bounded up the steps, his gun at the ready.

He entered through the front door, hoping all was well and Kinsley would greet him, but the house was quiet.

He whirled around when the door opened, preparing to fire if necessary. Kinsley stepped inside, her red hair blowing in the cold ocean wind and shut the door. Relief rushed through him. And fury. He lowered his weapon.

Her eyes grew wide. "Brett, I'm so sorry."

"Where did you go? I thought we agreed you wouldn't leave? Someone could have seen you."

"I know. I'm sorry. The elderly woman next door needed help finding her poodle, Cricket." Kinsley stepped forward. "I couldn't say no to that."

"I understand, but if Mrs. Taylor watches the news and sees your face, we're done. In fact, we probably need to leave." Brett moved to the windows to peer out. At least the blinds were still closed. "I think someone followed me in town, and it might not be long before they find me here—assuming they don't already know about this place. I have no idea if it's related to you, but I can't think of any other possibilities."

"How did they connect me to you so fast?"

"They could have spotted you last night in the homeless camp and followed us that way, but that doesn't make sense. If they had followed us to Camille's, I would have noticed the tail. Maybe the connection between us was made at the gas station, and that's all it took."

She stepped forward. "Oh, Brett. I'm so sorry. I didn't mean to put you in danger."

"I'm here to help, Kinsley. I wouldn't want you to go through this alone. I'm going to grab the bags so wait right here."

He went out the back of the house and kept to the area behind the rentals as he made his way to his vehicle, watching to make sure that the Subaru or any other suspicious vehicle wasn't in sight. He didn't see anything so he grabbed the purchases and made his way back to his rental house.

He tossed the sacks on the couch. "The sooner you can change your look, the better. Let me know if I can help you with…you know, dying your hair." *Though I really hate to see you change that beautiful hair color.*

"Thanks, Brett. If someone saw us together, you might need to change your look too."

And his vehicle.

In the master bath, he stared at the beard he'd grown. That had to go for now. Maybe his hair too? Nah. But he could trim his hair back to a shorter military style. Right now he was a scraggly lumberjack-looking guy. He finished changing his look, then got on his cell phone. He had some arrangements to make and was glad for all his connections, but the more connections he had to make—switch out his vehicle, use a safe house—the more chances his current operation would be discovered. He feared even contacting his siblings until he knew more. Ayden would be furious with Brett for jumping into the middle of this nightmare with both feet when he was supposed to be taking a break. Ayden didn't believe Brett could handle it—at least right now. More than that, with a mysterious law enforcement connection involved, any contact he made with HPS could compromise his and Kinsley's location, since HPS worked closely with law enforcement agencies.

Frustrated, Brett scraped a hand through his soon-to-be-cut cut hair.

Remaining low-key and under the radar was the best way to find answers for Kinsley and keep her safe. If only he could figure out how to guard his heart from falling for the woman with those big blue-green eyes all over again.

FIVE

Am I going overboard with this whole new look?

Maybe.

Great. She wasn't just talking to herself—she was answering herself now. She felt like everything that gave her stability and purpose had vanished, and she wasn't sure how to hold herself together. But she didn't have any other choice. She had to figure out from where the danger had come.

Who was the source of her terror? Who was responsible for Max's death? If changing her look would protect her for long enough to catch those men, then she'd do it—happily.

She glanced in the mirror at the pink cotton top Brett had purchased and the slim-fitting jeans. He'd pegged her size just right, but it had been a long time since she'd worn jeans. With one last look at her bobbed brown hair and her square glasses, she shrugged and exited the bathroom. She found Brett at the kitchen table with a cup of coffee—he looked entirely different and she stopped. Without the beard and scruffy hair he looked exactly like the guy she'd fallen in love with.

He stared at her as if stunned.

"What?" She ignored the sudden flutter of her heart and moved to the coffeepot to grab a fresh cup. "You don't like my new look?"

She cringed as she poured the coffee. She shouldn't care. She was almost sounding like the same person she'd been three years ago. It almost sounded like they were "them" again. A couple.

"You look great, Kinsley," he said. "I never doubted that you would, no matter the color of hair you had, with or without the glasses. Did I choose the wrong color? You should have given me some suggestions because, man, there must have been three thousand hair colors to choose from. A thousand shades for each color. Any look is great on you. Okay, I'm just going to stop talking now before I say something wrong."

He was cute. She chuckled as she turned and found him staring at her, but trying not to, just like she was trying not to take him in. Her heart just wouldn't slow down. With her glance to the living room—anywhere except Brett—she spotted his luggage. "Are you going somewhere?"

"*We're* going somewhere. There's the matter of Mrs. Taylor seeing you here. Add to that the fact that someone followed me this morning, and we need to move before they find us. I thought I already made that clear."

"You mentioned we probably need to leave, but I didn't realize it was a firm plan. But seriously, how do you know they haven't already found us?"

"I don't."

"Did you get the license plate number?"

"Someone got in my line of sight so I wasn't able to see. But I got a picture of him." Brett couldn't believe he'd forgotten. He slid his cell over with the image pulled up. "Do you recognize him?"

"No. Honestly, I think I got a good look at the men from the lab, but I was kind of dazed and the flames cast weird shadows. I'm saying he could have been there and, at this moment, I'm still not recognizing him. Does that sound weird?"

"Not at all."

She didn't believe him. "What are you going to do with that picture? Remember, we can't go to the police yet."

"I'm not sure, but I promise I won't talk to anyone until it's safe. We need to find out more. I know I said we'd go over this and brainstorm, but we can't do it here. We need to get out of here. Grab what you have and we'll leave. While I'm driving we'll talk more and try to figure out what's going on."

"That sounds like a plan." She only had her clothes from last night that had been through as much as she had, and the few new items that he'd bought her today. "I'll pay you back for everything, that is, once I get my hands on my wallet. I'm assuming the police have it, since I left it behind when I fled the scene."

She hoped the police were holding on to that for her instead of some criminal who could charge up her cards and deplete her bank account while she was in this precarious position. She wanted to second-guess her decision, but death had knocked too closely on her door, and that alone made her wary of approaching those who would normally be the first people to call. The police were usually where one would turn for help. And while she knew that was true for most of them, it wasn't true for at least one of them, and she couldn't take that risk. Not yet.

Knowing the stakes kept her focused and on track. She had to stay hidden until she was no longer in danger.

No more second-guessing.

After securing her few belongings in the small duffel Brett had been thoughtful enough to buy too, she slung it over her shoulder and met him at the door. He'd turned off all the lights and it didn't look like anyone had even stayed in this cute vacation rental.

An image flashed in her mind—she and Brett laughing and smiling and holding hands as they walked on the beach in some future that didn't exist, as a married couple staying in this bungalow. The thought caught her off guard, and she quickly pushed it to the far corners of her mind.

She followed him down the steps and hiked the path that weaved along the shore between the houses and the beach. The fog was lingering so she couldn't see much, but the wind had picked up and, even in the spring, it felt cold and brutal. But this was the Pacific Northwest, after all, and not sunny Southern California.

Still, Southern California had nothing on what she might see if the fog had gone—the sea stacks and rocky outcroppings were stunning.

Kinsley glanced over her shoulder and realized Brett's bungalow was almost out of sight. "The marine fog is really sticking to the coast this morning."

"That's a good thing. It helps keep us hidden." She climbed into the Highlander.

Had it been just last night that she'd been in the lab and talking to Max, and her world had been blown apart?

And Brett had been there for her.

She wouldn't forget his kindness, and that he was throwing away his vacation time to help *her.* Why would he do that? He backed from the parking spot and steered away from the homes, then up a long drive, stopping when he came to the main two-lane highway that hugged the coast. Highway 101 was the scenic route and for the most part hugged the west coast all the way from Southern California.

"Where are you taking us?"

"I think it's best to drive through the rain-forest—Olympic National Park—and head to Port Angeles. I'll make arrangements for us to stay there for the night and from there we can make our plans."

"You mean to figure out who is behind Max's death."

"And your attempted murder, don't forget."

"Don't worry. It's all fresh on my mind." *Too fresh.* Kinsley had grabbed a hoodie that Brett had purchased and slipped it on. She hugged herself and watched the lush foliage as they entered the rainforest in Olympic National Park.

"While we drive, it can't hurt to talk this through and see if we can come up with a reason that someone would want you and Max dead. Tell me about Max's personal life."

"He and my Dad were close, and he kind of

thought of himself as a father-figure to me after Dad died. But I wouldn't say I know everything about him. I do know that his wife died several years ago, before I started working for him. I think that's why he's a workaholic, so he won't have to miss her."

"Other family? Friends?"

"As far as I know, he only has one living relative, his aunt, Paula. Oh, Paula! Brett, I wish there was something I could do. That I could go comfort her and be there for her once she hears the news."

She pressed her face into her hands.

Brett gently squeezed her shoulder. "I'm sure that his aunt would want you to stay safe, Kinsley. You'll get the chance, don't worry."

She drew in a calming breath. She had to focus on staying safe and learning the truth about who killed Max. Still, her heart ached.

"Anyone else you can think of that was close to Max?"

"No one that I'm aware of."

"Okay. Well, the next thing that comes to mind to question is a sensitive project of some kind, but I really have no idea what that could be, so I'll let you fill me in."

Kinsley hadn't told Brett, but she still felt achy all over and could just close her eyes and go to sleep while he drove. Her head was starting to pound too, but worse than all of that was her heart. A dark cloud had settled in over her—*Max is dead.*

Gone.

"Just take your time, Kinsley. I know this is hard."

His tenderness made her smile inside. Once again she was glad she'd contacted him. She couldn't see herself going through this alone or with anyone else. Brett was perfect.

Except for the fact that the pain of their breakup echoed inside. But she had to ignore it.

"Max's lab is what we call a novel drug discovery lab or NMEs."

"Wait, what's an NME?"

"Oh, sorry. NME stands for new molecular entity." She gave a tired laugh. "I guess that doesn't help much. Basically, it's a chemical structure that has never been approved by the FDA before."

"So, a new drug to help people."

"Right. Exactly."

"Wow. That's something. And the fact someone took out his lab has me suddenly thinking of all kinds of conspiracy theories."

"I hope that's not it."

"Okay so the lab makes new drugs. What projects were you working on?"

Where did she even start? Better to keep it simple. "We were on the brink of a new novel drug discovery, or at least Max believed so. Max handled discovering the compounds and doing the initial tests to see if they had potential as treatment options. Once he'd isolated promising candidates, he'd pass them on to NewBio Scientific."

"NewBio Scientific? What's their role?"

"They're what's called a biopharma company. They're part of the drug discovery pipeline, including manufacturing once FDA approval is met."

"So Max was the one digging up the diamonds and then this other company polished them up and sold them?"

"Well…yeah, basically." It wasn't a perfect analogy, but it got the main message across.

"And Max had just found a big one?" Brett asked.

"Potentially," Kinsley agreed. "But the… polishing process takes a long time. The biggest moneymaker on the horizon is a new drug they're almost ready to bring to market. They've invested a lot into it. The process requires millions of dollars and FDA approval."

"Whoa…millions of dollars? I guess I knew that, but when you're talking that kind of money, those conspiracy theories start to make more sense."

A chill crawled over her, and she hugged

herself tighter as the road twisted and turned through the rainforest.

"It's a big-ticket business. It's not cheap to create new drugs, but the potential profits are huge."

"Anything more you can tell me, preferably in English." He chuckled. "Who did you work with at NewBio? Would they have any reason to harm you or Max?"

"Max interacted with NewBio, not me. And I can't think of any reason they'd have to want to harm us. We were making them money, after all. But maybe there's something else involved that I'm not aware of. The entire process is long and complicated, and I just focus on my research in the lab." Which was too complicated to explain to Brett so she wouldn't bother.

"Tell me about Max. Did he say anything that made you suspicious in the weeks leading up to the explosion?" He arched a brow.

"No, nothing. That night, though, he'd just come back from exploring caves and gathering samples. He was acting kind of strange when he got to the lab. Kind of excited and yet stressed.'"

"Hmm. Maybe that's something to look into."

"How, Brett? How exactly can we look into it? We can't talk to Max." Her voice shook and she stared out the window, hiding the tears from Brett.

* * *

As Brett finally steered them into Port Angeles on the Washington Peninsula, he kept a sharp eye out for the Subaru or any other possible followers. He couldn't fathom that someone had already found them—but someone clearly had. For that reason, he shouldn't be surprised if it happened again. At any rate, he would remain wary and be on the lookout.

During the drive, talking about the lab had upset Kinsley so he'd left off with the rest of the questions. But something bothered him—someone could have been after Max for personal reasons that had nothing at all to do with the lab, except for the fact that Kinsley had been included in the bombing. That indicated that this was connected to their work, but who would benefit from seeing it stopped?

After checking them in, he found a parking spot near the entrance, and he led her to their adjoining rooms down the long hallway. Olympic Inn sat up on a hill overlooking the town and the Pacific Ocean, more specifically the Strait of Juan de Fuca that separated Washington from Canada.

Once they were in their second-floor hotel rooms, Kinsley opened up the window to let the fresh air in and look out. The clouds had moved out to reveal a beautiful blue-sky day. Even the water sparkled from the strait.

"It's beautiful," she said. "The fog burned off and…it's breathtaking."

Yeah, he kind of thought so too, but Kinsley was more beautiful by far, and he was struggling to breathe for a different reason. No matter her hairstyle, she was stunning. Not only was she beautiful, she was brilliant. She was passionate and caring. She turned to look at him as if she might have guessed what he was thinking.

I sure hope not.

"I'm sorry I dragged you into this mess, Brett. You're hiding a fugitive now. A fugitive from the law."

Yeah. Maybe. Then again, maybe not. "Don't think like that. You're not running from the law. You're hiding from a killer. For all we know, the police could be concerned that you've been abducted. You mentioned leaving your wallet in your vehicle. That they want to find you and talk to you makes sense. Don't automatically think the worst." He joined her at the window and tugged the curtains closed. "As beautiful as the view is, I think it's best if we keep the curtain closed."

"Do you think someone followed you again?" Kinsley opened the drawers on each of the side tables and the desk drawer. She pulled out the hotel information but didn't look at it. She seemed to be fidgeting.

Because she was alone with him? "I don't want to take any chances."

Kinsley leaned against the desk and lifted her blue-green gaze to him. "What next?"

What next was such an open-ended question and ignited a larger question in his mind—what next with Kinsley after this was over. But he shut those thoughts down. There was no "with Kinsley" for him on the other side of this.

He steadied his voice. "We stay the night while I work on some things."

"What things?"

Yeah. He was kind of afraid she might ask. No matter his hesitation to contact his siblings—mainly Ayden, older brother and company founder—eventually he was going to have to do just that. There was no getting around it. HPS could protect Kinsley and work out how she could cooperate with the police in a safe way and out of reach of the attacker with a connection inside the local PD. But doing that would be tricky.

And he wouldn't bring HPS into this until he knew enough to make sure he could do it without compromising her safety. Plus, Kinsley might consider Honor Protection Specialists to be too close to the authorities. They were certainly connected and worked with multiple law enforcement agencies. She'd told him not to contact the authorities—and she had her reasons. Good reasons.

He was afraid that as soon as she found out he worked with HPS, she might disappear on him. He would need to persuade her they could help—when the time was right.

"I'm working on an idea." He shrugged. "I'll let you know more when I've figured it out."

Kinsley narrowed her eyes. "I'm not sure I like the sound of that. I need to know what's going on."

"Well, first, I'm going to town to buy a laptop that you can use to connect to your lab data to get results and try to find answers to who would have wanted to kill Max and why."

He almost held his breath as he waited for her reaction.

Her shoulders relaxed. "I guess that's a good start. Yeah, sure. I can log into my account remotely. But *they* might be watching for that."

"They might." He hoped to chat with Everly and see if she could set things up so they weren't exactly traceable. She was their computer specialist, and she owed him a favor. So he could get her assistance with assurances that she wouldn't ask questions or report in to Ayden. She wouldn't like it.

"So just relax here while I go. There's a stocked mini fridge. Anything I can get you while I'm out."

Kinsley dug through the duffel bag he'd bought her.

"You'll be okay here alone for a few minutes, won't you?"

She zipped up the duffel one-handed. "No. I won't. That's why I'm going with you."

"I don't think that's a good idea."

"I'm in my disguise, and I don't want to be alone. Someone might knock on the door and ask me to help them find their lost dog." Her smile was endearing.

"Okay. We're going to walk to town, though. I need to secure a different vehicle. Are you good for that?"

"Yeah."

He'd planned to talk to Everly while Kinsley was in the hotel room, but with her along, there was no hiding his plans.

"Something else…" Oh, boy. "I need to tell you about what I've been up to."

"Oh?" Kinsley angled her face, her eyes wary.

"Well, I know you're not in the Coast Guard anymore."

"You do? How do you know?"

"I thought you would have figured it out by

now. I mean, how else would I find your phone number?"

He'd wondered about that, but he hadn't thought it through long enough to come to that conclusion. Brett wasn't entirely sure how he felt about that, but he smiled. "Okay so you know I work with my siblings at Honor Protection Specialists."

"Yes, I knew that." Her face turned pink. "I hope you're not mad."

"Why would I be mad?" A measure of relief filled him that she already knew about HPS. They exited the hotel and started down the hill. Brett kept an eye out for the Subaru or anyone else who might follow or track them.

"I hope you're not mad that I'm going to hold your hand now like we're a couple to anyone watching the news. It's part of the disguise. It that okay?" Otherwise, maybe walking wasn't a good idea. But the Subaru driver was looking for Brett and Kinsley and right now, they weren't looking like those people.

She reached for his hand and he took it. His heart rate inched up at her touch. "I hope you're not getting in over your head, Brett?"

Oh, yeah. I'm in over my head all right.

SIX

Brett finally released her hand at the car rental place. "I'm renting a car. You can take a seat inside."

"I'm not smart about this stuff, but with the hotel and now a car, if these people who killed Max have any connections and are looking for you, can't they track your activity?"

"If they're looking for me, which they probably are, I highly doubt that I've been connected to you yet. But if they were, I'm not using my regular card."

"What. You're using an alias? A fake ID?"

"No. I used a burner credit card. There are ways to do it to keep your privacy. I used an alias post office box for my address. I also already reserved a rental via an app. I'm not new to this."

"Oh, I get it. In protection services you want to keep what you're doing private."

"To protect my clients, yes."

"And I'm getting your services for free. I'll make it up to you, Brett. I'll pay you."

He drew closer, and she could smell his musky masculine scent. Unfortunately, that made her head kind of fuzzy.

"I'm doing this on my own time. I'm helping you because I want to. HPS isn't involved."

A knot lodged in her throat. She had a feeling that Brett wanted them involved, though. "Good. Because I'm not sure I'm ready to trust anyone else just yet. I know they have to work closely with law enforcement. They can't obstruct justice. That sort of thing. I just… I keep envisioning being taken into custody or for questioning—whatever—and the inside cop, whoever he or she is, comes in to kill me and finishes the job." With the words, Kinsley shook uncontrollably.

Brett gently gripped her arms. Held her gaze. "That's not going to happen. I won't let that happen."

She stared into his eyes. Wanted to believe him. But how could he make that promise? The thing was, she'd trusted Brett enough to call him—in her desperation—even knowing about HPS.

"I won't bring HPS in on this until you agree," he said.

She had to calm her pounding heart. He finally stepped away

She drew in a breath. "Thank you."

He stared at her long and hard. "You're welcome." A few heartbeats later, he added, "Are you ready for the next step in this plan?"

"Let's do it."

"I won't ask you to wait outside, but when you come in, just sit in the chair. I'll go to the counter and get the vehicle."

"Okay." Inside the car rental place, Brett moved to the counter, and like he had asked, she took a chair near the window.

She wished she hadn't insisted on coming with Brett. She felt completely exposed, despite her disguise.

A Port Angeles police cruiser slowly drove by and Kinsley reflexively shrunk away from the window. She felt like a criminal when she wasn't. Brett grabbed her elbow and urged her outside and to their rental vehicle—a compact cargo van.

She stopped in her tracks. "What's this?"

"Nobody is going to look twice at this." Brett opened the door for her.

Half laughing, she got in.

After he started the van up, he pulled out of the parking lot. "Now to get the laptop and anything else we need."

"What about your vehicle at the hotel?" The pretty coastal town surrounding her did nothing to calm her fears.

"I rented the room for a few days." He turned right at a light.

What? "We're not staying here, are we?"

"We'll figure out what we're doing next," he said, "but my vehicle will remain parked while I have the hotel room. We need to do some digging, Kinsley, don't you think?"

"Brett, I saw a police cruiser driving slowly by earlier. You don't think they're looking for me, do you?" She hugged herself.

"You're missing, so yes."

"I'm scared. What if they find me?"

"I won't let that happen." He shot her a reassuring look.

"But this could get you into trouble."

"Listen, Kinsley, let's find out what we can. Your life is what's important here. I'm in this with you no matter what."

I'm in this with you.

Why did he have to say that? He'd said those words to her long ago on one of the rare stretches of time they'd had together back when they were long-distance dating. She'd been concerned that it couldn't last, but he'd looked at her with such tenderness, such love, and said, "I'm in this with you."

Until he wasn't.

The same could be said for this situation. Brett Honor was a good man, but he could only keep up this charade with her for so long.

"Look out!" she screamed. A blue vehicle headed straight for them.

The Subaru!

The vehicle nearly hit them but swerved at the last moment, then kept going. Heart pounding, Brett kept driving. That had been close. It wasn't the first time he'd had a near-miss traffic collision. But it was the first time it had happened with someone he'd been trying to lose.

What was going on? The driver hadn't intended to ram them but had definitely been speeding. "I don't think he was targeting us. I don't think he knows we're in the van."

"You don't think who targeted us?"

"That's the man who followed me back from town. But he obviously knows we're here. Unless…he opted to search for us north instead of south on the main road through the peninsula."

"So you're saying that just because he is here, doesn't mean he knows that we're here yet."

"He could have been driving around searching, and he guessed correctly that we'd stop at the next town along the way." He didn't like this at all. Maybe they should have stopped off at a campsite, but he wasn't prepared for camping in this area when it was still cold.

Brett turned off into a parking lot and stopped.

"What are you thinking?"

"That I need you to get in the back of the van for starters. I don't want anyone to see you right now."

"But I have a disguise. We're in this van that no one would associate with either one of us. He drove right past us because of that."

"Please, Kinsley—I'd feel better if you got in the back."

Kinsley unbuckled, then scrambled into the back seat. "I thought we were going to get a laptop. Looks like you're turning around."

"I'm following the Subaru from a distance. The license plate number is YYB4366. Text me that number."

His cell dinged, letting him know he'd just gotten a text. "Thanks."

"No problem. Where do you think he's going?"

"I hate to say it but looks like he is going to the hotel. He's parking down the street." *Which might mean I've been an idiot and need to get rid of my cell for now too.* This guy had gotten a lot done in a short time. It wasn't a stretch to think that he must know Brett's identity now and had followed his cell phone's signal.

"What are you going to do?"

I'd like to approach him and punch out his lights after I ask him some questions.

"I'm going to remove the SIM card from my cell. I can't think how else he might have followed me. I guess I'm surprised he figured me out so soon."

Brett turned off his cell, then removed the SIM card. "Can you hand me the box with the other burner cell? I'm glad I bought two. Too bad I didn't think to switch over sooner. Plug your number into it—and text me that license plate number again." Nothing was more important than staying connected to Kinsley.

"Here you go." She handed the burner cell forward and Brett saw that she'd found his new cell number and texted hers, along with the license plate info.

"I'm going to try to get to our room and get our things and come out the back. You just stay inside the van. We can stay on the cell together and if you see any movement or any suspicious activity let me know. But no one should see you hiding in the van, okay?" He was more than relieved he'd used a burner credit card.

He'd made a mistake not using the burner cell too, unless…

"Are you sure he found you via your cell phone?"

"If he didn't, then he must be the police officer or have connections to the local police. If that's the case, then he knew about my car, and he has put a BOLO out on you." Still, that was some fancy police work to find them so quickly. "At any rate, something sure seems fishy."

Ayden or Everly would let him know if that kind of alert had been triggered on him.

He needed to make a decision on how to handle this precarious situation since he was part of a security consultants' group. Could this be any more awkward? "You good to stay inside the van?"

"I changed my disguise and still have to hide. I'm okay, yes, but please hurry."

"You know what? Forget it. Nothing in our room is worth the risk. We can get more clothes. Get everything else we need later. Our room is rented out and no one is going to mess with it."

Kinsley released a sigh.

"I can tell you're relieved." He squeezed the steering wheel but didn't start the van. "I think I should go ahead and talk to this guy and find out why he's following me. If I get his name, then we'll know something."

"What if he's a cop, Brett? You'll have to turn me over to him." Fear edged her tone.

"Don't worry. I won't be turning you over. If he's law enforcement, then he's the dirty cop connection."

"How can you know that?"

"If he was with law enforcement, you would already be taken in for questioning. Ayden or Everly would already have heard from our law enforceement connections about my involvement, and they would contact me. No, this guy, whoever he is, is working in the shadows and under the radar."

"I hope you're right"

"If I talk to him, then maybe we can connect the dots and learn more about who is behind the bombing. He still doesn't know about this van, so I'll get some answers, then we can leave. In fact, you can drive the van out of here, that way he won't connect the vehicle to me and it'll still be safe for you."

"I'm not sure about this, Brett, but you know more about what you're doing in this scenario than I could ever know." She slipped into the front seat and grabbed his arm. "Please be careful."

Brett could look in her blue-green eyes forever. He'd been such an idiot to push the best thing in his life away.

Without thinking, he grabbed her hand and squeezed. He only wanted to reassure her, but a spark of attraction surged up his arm. He released her hand. "I'm heading out. Just hide in the van. Keep the doors locked. I'll be right back."

"Can we move the van so I can at least watch what's going on?"

"That would be too risky. I don't want him to know about the van. I'll come out of the hotel as I approach him, and then I'll go back in, and come out the back to get in the van and we'll leave. If I'm not back in ten minutes..."

"If you're not back what?"

"If I'm not back in ten minutes, you should go."

"Go where?" Her eyes widened. "Brett, maybe this isn't such a good idea."

"Look, I need to do this. We know someone is behind it. Finding out who that is will help keep you safe. I can't promise I'll be able to get this guy to talk, but I have to at least try."

"What if you confront that guy, and all the evidence disappears? They'll know we're onto them. I'd prefer to find out what I need to know before they realize I heard their conversation."

"That's a good point. But I think the fact that you disappeared, you're missing and you haven't gone to the police clues them in."

She pursed her lips and looked away. "Okay. So go. Just go. Ten minutes is all you get."

He would make it five, just in case.

He hopped out and rushed through the back door of the hotel using his keycard, then hurried through the front door, hoping that this wasn't a big mistake. But how could he let this opportunity get away from him?

Skirting the parking lot, he took the sidewalk, and, in his peripheral vision, noted the guy still sitting in the car. So he was just going to follow them and nothing more? Brett had to do this. He'd committed to protecting Kinsley and helping her get answers.

He started across the street, but the guy suddenly peeled away from the curb and took off.

"Hey!" Brett threw his hands up. "I just want to talk."

Now he would have to keep an even sharper eye out. Their follower could get a new vehicle too, or someone else could do the following. Either way, someone was definitely interested in Kinsley for what she knew or what she didn't know—and until he and Kinsley figured out who was behind this, they wouldn't be able to see the danger coming.

SEVEN

Kinsley followed Brett into their new hotel in a suburb just south of Seattle. They'd taken the ferry across Puget Sound. By the time they got to their destination, the day was nearly over, and Kinsley was dead on her feet.

Inside their connected rooms, Kinsley plopped into a chair, closed her eyes and leaned her head back to rest. "I feel like this is all a waste of time and we haven't accomplished anything."

"Before we can make any real headway, you have to be safe." Brett pulled bottled water from the fridge in the kitchenette and offered her one.

She took it and almost drank the whole bottle, then got up and paced.

Brett was looking at her. *I must look a mess.*

She ran her hand through her hair and then gasped before remembering that she'd cut it. Why hadn't she just worn a wig instead?

"And it wasn't a waste of time. Look." Brett gestured at the desk in her room.

She stepped in and stopped. "A laptop. What? How?" She didn't like where this was going.

He held his hands up. "Everly owes me plenty of favors. She arranged for the rooms under an alias and set up this laptop—without asking a single question. She knows nothing about you. She did this for me. She'll want answers later."

"When did you have time to ask her?"

"I stopped for gas. You'd fallen asleep, and I texted her my new number and made my request. This laptop is untraceable via a masked IP address or some such thing—that's her department. You can feel safe diving into the data at your lab. Grab as much as you can in case you get locked out by someone else who has access."

She nodded and approached the laptop. "It's all set up and everything?"

"Yes. Everly provided a USB drive as well, so connect that and you can download information you need. That is, if there's anything to find."

"And that's what I don't know. I don't know what I'm looking for."

"Maybe I could have Everly do this. She's good at..."

"I can't ask her to do that. She wouldn't know what she's looking at either. I feel like I'm messing with evidence. Besides, I signed nondisclosure agreements when Max hired me. I'm not supposed to share the lab's data with anyone who isn't authorized." She paused. "Though with his death and his research at risk, I'm not sure that matters anymore. And though Max's lab was destroyed, the data is both processed and stored at an off-site server with an IT company servicing pharmaceutical companies."

"If the police are doing their job investigating the explosion, then they are securing evidence, including forensic and computer evidence that could explain what happened. But the warrant to secure this kind of data will take them time. There's something else. I wasn't sure how to tell you this…"

"What is it?" Kinsley held her breath.

"Well, Everly said they believe the explosion was caused by a chemical reaction. They might have considered it an accident. Except—"

"I'm missing. Kinsley paced the small space, then jerked her head up to him. Brett, if you didn't tell Everly about me, then why is she discussing anything with you?"

"Because she saw the news and your name on it—she knew we were together before, of course."

"And if she connected me to you, then others might."

"Our being together wasn't public knowledge. But the simple fact that someone followed us means they already know you're with me now.

I'm sure someone ran my license plate number or tracked my cell. But we're operating under the identity radar right now. Everly's has done that for me, though she doesn't know about you."

"It's only a matter of time before she figures out that your current operation involves me."

"Maybe so. But right now, she didn't sound like she knew. And I suspect she hasn't learned because whoever is following us is probably connected to the police officer connected to the man who's behind Max's murder. I'm saying the search for me, isn't going across the police channels."

Kinsley sat at the desk. "And right now, they're keeping that information under wraps because they want to get to me before the good guy police."

"But there could come a point where the police are looking for me too in order to bring you in."

"And once I'm in custody—" *I'm in danger. I could die. He is going to kill me.*

If only she knew who "he" was.

Brett took two steps forward to stand closer. Maybe too close, but then again, she appreciated his reassurance. Kinsley wanted to lean into him, but she kept to herself.

"I won't let it come to that," he said. "I promise." He looked at her, and she had the feeling he wanted to hug her to him. Instead, he glanced behind her then back. "Do you need to sleep awhile before you work?"

"I look that bad, huh?"

He looked her over and then his grin was adorable. "No. Of course, not, but I can tell you're exhausted. A little rest might do you good. It could help you see things clearly when you finally get to work."

She sighed. "I won't be able to sleep soundly until this is over." She eyed the bathroom. *I'd really love to brush my teeth and my hair and freshen up.* "What about clothes and toiletries? We left those at the other place. You could get those items while I work."

"My amazing sister stocked us up."

Uh-oh. "What?"

"It's what we do at HPS. She's used to it."

"Brett, you said she doesn't know about me."

"We've been over this. She doesn't know this is about *you*, specifically. She has no idea what I'm doing."

"She's not stupid."

"Exactly. Anything she thinks she knows will not leave her mouth."

Right. He was covering for Everly. He knew good and well his sister had probably put two and two together. "Can I ask you something?"

"Ask away." He pursed his lips.

She almost laughed at his expression. "You want to tell them, don't you?"

Scrunching his face, he scratched the back of his neck. "Them? You mean my siblings?"

"Yes. You want them involved."

He blew out a breath. "I do. Of course, I do. I don't want to leave you exposed. Yes, we protect people but we usually don't have to protect them from the police. But I've already told you, I won't tell them until you're ready and it's safe."

Kinsley took the chair at the desk. She needed to relax and trust him. Brett got it. He understood her. They were on the same page. Bringing in the police before she had evidence could get them both killed, and no one brought to justice. Not that he thought his family would force her to go to the police, of course, but this being an active investigation, neither could they harbor a fugitive, hide evidence or obstruct justice.

But Brett would do what he must to protect Kinsley.

"Thank you for sticking with me, even though it means not being open with your family of co-workers."

He took the other chair. "You have to believe that this is all going to work out. We'll figure it out. At some point, though, we might have no choice but to bring in Honor Protection Specialists. Will you trust me to know when that is?"

I don't know! She said nothing. What could she say?

His half smile flattened. "It's okay. Think about it. I'm going to whip us up some grub in the kitchenette while you work."

"That sounds good." Everly had bought food too?

He got up and headed for the kitchen. She could read the disappointment in his demeanor. Why did it bother her so much?

She followed him and wanted to reach out and press her hand against his strong back. He had the broadest shoulders. "Listen… Brett… I'm not sure I trust you to know when it is, okay? I'm not sure I trust *myself* to know. Let's just make sure we talk about it as we go. Maybe together we'll know if we *can* bring them in. I'm just not convinced that's going to happen."

Weirdly he didn't frown, but instead nodded and gave her a tenuous smile. "I'm glad you're still honest."

He reached into the fridge and pulled out eggs. "Is an omelet okay?"

"I'm impressed that she stocked the fridge."

"Yep. She loves this part of helping others— making sure they're comfortable in their new surroundings."

"I never got to meet her. And would love to meet her now, but under different circum-

stances." Now why had she said that? Bringing
it up was dragging up their past and pulling it
into their present.

Brett said nothing. She left him to work.
Eggs cracked behind her and soon the aroma
of food filled the rooms. She booted up the laptop, gained access with the generic passcode left
on a sticky note and finally logged into the lab
to peruse reports and data.

*If there's something in these reports to trig-
ger murder, God, please help me find it.*

Kinsley was skimming through the hundreds
of reports created in the last several years, and
focused on those over the last month. Brett set
an omelet next to her on the desk along with
a glass of sparkling water with lemon. That
caught her attention.

He remembered?

And had Everly bought that per his request?
Or was it just a coincidence?

He pulled up a chair and held his plate. "Let's
say grace and then we can eat."

That he still believed and practiced his faith
warmed her heart. After he said grace, the hun-
ger actually kicked in, even though minutes before she hadn't thought she could eat yet.

"While we eat, why don't you tell me more
about Max's drug discovery company? How
does his company compare to others?"

"Good question." She took a bite of the eggs. "You make a mean omelet."

"Don't get your hopes up. That's all I can make."

"Not true. You made an amazing spaghetti Bolognese a couple of times. Oh, I'd love to have a plate of that now." Oh, no. Again? She needed to divert this conversation before she ended up asking him why. *Why did you break things off with me?* I thought we were in love...

"You asked about other companies like Max's. There aren't a lot, actually. Max searched for natural products to facilitate new drugs. The mainstream drug companies have considered that process to take too long. Finding new drugs from nature supposedly offers limited discoveries. Big Pharma finds new drugs by comparing and testing thousands of synthetics in their search for biological activity. Thousands can be tested every month compared to Max who might uncover one or two natural candidates for a new drug once a month."

Brett released a heavy exhale. "Wow. I see the comparison. But why'd he go this route then instead of joining the rest?"

She shrugged. "He's more interested in the uniqueness of the project. I guess I should say he was interested." Grief hit her all over again. But she pushed it aside for the moment. If she was going to get justice for Max, she has to push through. "He was more interested in being different. He was inspired by a researcher in Tennessee and followed in his path. The search for specific bacteria from the colonies found in caves is complicated. Once Max found specimens that were good candidates, he then grew the isolated microbes, extracts potential compounds and put those through tests."

Brett gave her a small smile, and she could tell she was losing him. At least his eyes hadn't glazed over.

"To find what?" he asked.

Nice. He wanted more. "Potential drug activity."

"How does that happen?"

She could smile at his interest, but then she reminded herself this is about finding the truth about Max's murder. "Special equipment and software were developed for the purpose."

"Special—as in unique."

"Yes."

"And he must have a decent success rate or else he couldn't stay in business."

"Right. Initially Max worked off grants until he partnered with NewBio, he got funding for his research through them. The hard part is finding a compound that is completely new— hence novel drug discovery."

"So, let's say Max discovered a new compound that got someone's attention. The *wrong* someone's attention." He frowned and slightly shook his head.

She chuckled to herself. "You're doing great with the questions."

"You mean considering I have no idea what you're talking about?"

"I'm trying to speak English and I think you're doing well. The point is we find Max's killer. As to your theory, Max found two compounds that NewBio is in the process of bringing to market. One is a new cancer treatment, and the other one is an antiviral. Both drugs have the potential to make NewBio millions of dollars—and that's a conservative estimate."

"And Max?"

"It would mean Max is paid a substantial amount for his work in addition to the research already funded.I should say...*would have* been paid."

Brett hung his head for a few moments, then, frowning, took her plate and headed to the kitchenette. "I'll let you get to work. Let me know if you find anything suspicious."

Everly had also set Brett up with his own laptop so he could scour the news and research on his own. There was really no way that she didn't know he was working with Kinsley, but right now, neither of them was talking about it.

And he knew he could count on her to keep it to herself. Ayden and Caine might be furious on the other side of this, then again, they would both understand the need for secrecy to protect all parties, considering HPS worked closely with the police and someone was working with the murderer from inside the police department. A report or comment or memo could be seen by the wrong person. That's all Brett was doing now, protecting Kinsley.

Brett completely trusted his siblings, even to understand when he was struggling. He'd been alone at the vacation rental house, keeping to himself, when he was supposed to be on a sunny beach somewhere in Fiji. Oh, well, he preferred to stay in the North Pacific.

And he was glad he hadn't gone south. Who would Kinsley have turned to otherwise? She didn't seem to have anyone else. And he had to admit that helping her pulled the focus off himself and was exactly what he needed to pull him out of his funk because of the PTSD he was loath to admit he had after the helicopter crash.

Brett *needed* Kinsley, or at least to help her. He shouldn't start thinking he needed her in a personal way, though. But man, even with her new look he could easily find himself smitten if he wasn't careful. Her short brown hair had replaced the luscious long red hair and had now made her blue-green eyes appear to take on a completely different color. They were emerald sometimes. Turquoise others. It reminded him of the first time he'd seen her. He'd been assisting on the rescue helicopter to help her family out of a region that had flooded, and her eyes had caught his attention.

Somehow, he had to stop thinking about her, had to stop remembering their past and how they met and how he'd felt about her before. He couldn't think about that. He couldn't think about his stupidity in ending things with her. He was damaged goods, and she wouldn't want him back. Nor would he do that to her.

He finished cleaning up the small mess he'd made, then hung the dishrag to dry.

"Brett?" Kinsley called through the open door between their rooms.

He entered her room and found her staring at her computer. It looked like she'd found something. He looked over her shoulder at the computer screen.

"Over the last many weeks Max had set what he calls traps in a cave. It's covered with a membrane and the goal is to see which bacteria cut through the membranes to live inside the wafer. He collected two the night the lab blew up, but the week before he'd collected a few wafers and had written up a report."

"And?"

"Well, there's so much more that goes into this process."

"I know that I'm not going to understand most of what you're talking about, but please just tell me—what did you find?"

"That's just it. It's not what I found, but rather what I didn't find. He writes reports on everything. His reports from his collections over the last two weeks are missing."

Brett waited. He could tell she was formulating an idea and had more to say. But he had an idea too that he would pass on to Everly. Whoever had access to those missing reports could be involved or have answers.

"I think I need to take a look at the cave from where he's collecting this new material."

Brett's breath caught. He hadn't expected that. "What do you think you could find in a cave that could help us to know who is behind his death?"

"I just think it's weird he was visiting a cave and collecting specimens, and then the lab blows up and those reports are gone. I think it's good detective work to at least go to the cave and see where he left the traps. Get any he might have left behind. Wouldn't you agree?"

He nodded. "This wouldn't have been my first thought, but you make a good point with that."

"And there's another thing. If I'm going to collect the traps he set and look at what he might have discovered, I'll need lab equipment."

"But you said the lab equipment and software he used are unique and especially developed for his process."

"They are, but I can still do some of the work."

He had to think about this. Brett wasn't entirely sure this would get them anywhere. *But what do I know?* Nothing. "Do you happen to know where we could secure equipment you could use?"

"The local university with a biochemical program. I can replicate at least some of what he was doing." She angled her head. "Do you think your sister can arrange this for me?"

"Are you saying you trust her to know you're involved?"

"I don't see what choice I have—but do *you* trust her?"

Brett couldn't help the small smile. Now they were getting somewhere. "Completely."

"Besides, we both know that Everly must realize I'm the person you're helping," Kinsley said. "I don't have to like it, but here we are."

"I'm glad you're letting me bring her in on this officially, though quietly."

"You said it. Quietly. Just between you, me and Everly. Just because she knows, doesn't mean I want HPS in this officially."

"While she's on it, let's have Everly follow the money and also look into Max's past. Maybe someone had a grudge. She could look for anomalies, while we work on this angle. We need this help, Kinsley. We can't do it all." He paused, gauging her reaction. "You look like you have more to say. Did you find something else?"

"No. But I need some supplies before we go to the cave. Though we won't need actual hardcore spelunking equipment, we'll need the usual flashlight and helmet, surgical gloves, and I'll need collection tubes."

"Everly is going to love this." He doubted she'd ever had such an intriguing assignment.

"I'm glad someone does."

He winced. "I'm sorry. That was a ridiculously insensitive thing for me to say. Max lost his life, and I shouldn't—"

She gave him a weak smile. "No worries, Brett. I understand what you meant. I didn't mean to snap at you. I think I should get some sleep, after all. My brain is turning to oatmeal. But if your sister can arrange the lab and the supplies, we can travel to the cave tomorrow. I want to look at the science behind this while we also investigate Max's death. Max's murder."

"Don't forget your attempted murder," Brett pulled the chair up close while she shut the laptop. He leveled his gaze on her to make sure she was paying attention. "Are you sure about this cave? Is it safe? Is there any reason someone else might be there too? Any reason at all?"

"I don't have the answer to that question. But if I can find the traps he left behind and gather data, working backward, maybe I can learn what he learned that could have been worth his life. Our lives. It could be that a competitor didn't want him to make the discovery that would be in direct competition with a new drug coming on the market. It's a start. "I can't imagine whoever is behind this would completely destroy the data."

"Whoever is behind his death probably already has the information, but we won't know what that is since it's all gone from the server. I don't know if Max scrubbed it or if someone else deleted the files."

She stood, then stretched and yawned.

Kinsley was the most beautiful woman he'd ever met. And on the inside, she had an amazing warm and caring heart. And if that wasn't enough, she was also the most brilliant person he knew. *Sorry, Everly.*

Brett had to watch himself around her. He stood to exit her room and give her space to rest. "Good night, Kinsley. I'll be just next door. I'm leaving the door cracked. Let me know if you need anything at all. I'm right there. I'll try to be quiet while I make arrangements with Everly." He couldn't tear his gaze away, and apparently, he had all kinds of excuses to stand there and look at her.

She walked to the door separating the rooms and gestured for him to leave, then partially closed the door. "Good night, Brett."

See you tomorrow, Kinsley.

He couldn't help but think this was some kind of providential second chance with her.

A chance he couldn't take. He'd messed up with her before because he was damaged.

And nothing about that had changed.

EIGHT

At the parking lot to the cave entrance—a lava tube near Mt. St. Helens—Brett emerged from the woods and approached the van, signaling she could get out.

Opening the door, Kinsley slid out. *I can't believe I'm doing this.* In her lab, observing microorganisms, it was quiet and safe. She hadn't done anything so bold in years. Bold, as in facing potential danger to find a murderer.

In the higher elevation, the spring air was cold. Wearing a beanie and puffing out white clouds Brett approached, breathless and smelling of woods and fresh air.

"Looks like we're alone today so far. Even if another group of tourists arrive, as long as they're not connected to Max's murder, we'll be okay. Let's get this done and over with so we can get out of here."

She understood his urgency, but this would take them time, and she didn't want to rush.

Wearing packs filled with supplies, they donned helmets with lights and grabbed their flashlights. The cave would be pitch-black in places. In her sturdy hiking boots and jacket, Kinsley led the way down the steps as if she knew what she was doing. She hadn't been to this particular cave with Max.

At the yawning maw of the cave, they stopped to read the sign. "Gotta act like tourists," she whispered.

One of the emphasized rules—*Do not touch cave walls—touch kills the slime.*

"Cave slime. That's what Max collected, isn't it?" Brett asked.

She led him down a stairwell into the dark hole until the steps ended. "In answer to your question, yes and no. He collected the creatures that eat the slime. And while he does it, he wears—um, wore—protective gloves to get what he needed. I'll do the same, so technically, it's not like I'll be touching it."

They continued along the worn path inside the cave.

"And how exactly did he get away without touching the slime, collecting it, if it's against the rules."

The light from the entrance was quickly fading and chills crawled over her. *Am I making a mistake?*

"Yeah. About that. Max is considered a researcher and had special access and permissions afforded scientists."

Her voice sounded weird bouncing off walls. Basaltic lava—not something usually seen in the Cascade Range of volcanoes, Max had explained, although it was common in Hawaii.

The lava tube grew increasingly dark until it was pitch-black. Even with her headlamp, she stumbled on the rough path of rocks and pebbles.

"Where exactly in the cave did he do this research? Leave these traps to collect microorganisms?" Brett asked.

"That's a good question."

"What? You mean you don't know?"

"We'll have to explore the cave and look for protected areas. I don't think anyone would notice the wafer traps he set and I believe they should remain where he left them. He usually arranged to collect bacteria in a cordoned off portion of the cave. I just don't know where that is in this cave."

Brett remained quiet behind her as he followed, then finally asked, "Why didn't you tell me?"

"What? That we might have to explore the entire lava tube to find what I'm looking for?"

"Yes. That."

"I think you know the answer. Funny thing about Max. He talked too much. He loved giving the details and, who knows, maybe he said something to the wrong person and that's what got him killed. Even so, he never gave me details about where he was specifically collecting specimens."

"Do you think that was odd?" he asked.

"I didn't think so until now. But maybe I'm just overanalyzing things."

"Maybe." Brett hesitated to go farther. "I wonder if we could be in the wrong cave?"

"You need to relax, Brett. This will take time. And yes, it's possible we're in the wrong cave, but I don't think so." She moved her head to shine the light around, then huffed when she spotted the rock pile blocking their path. But she'd read about that in the website information about the cave so knew to expect it.

"There's no way around it, so we'll need to go over it."

She wouldn't tell Brett how unprepared for this kind of physical exertion she was, but he would figure that out on his own eventually. She spent most of her time in the lab or at home.

Home. Lab. Home. Lab.

I really need to get a life. That is, after this was over. Brett scaled the rocks and at the top, he glanced back down at her. "Watch out for that slippery portion."

"I discovered it already, but thanks."

He reached for her, and she offered her hand so he could assist her the rest of the way. Then they scaled the other side of the pile together. "I'm glad we're wearing gloves. These lava rocks are sharp."

Kinsley was glad to plant her feet on the ground, even though inside a lava tube it was always going to be rough and treacherous. Still, she was the one leading the way, and they moved deeper, searching for what Max had left behind. Evidence that he'd been here.

About a half mile in, the cave grew narrow, and the hardened lava flowed downward quite a few feet. She couldn't see just how far, but it looked like a black, frozen waterfall.

"What are you doing?" Brett asked. "Are we really going down that? Is that even allowed?"

"I read about it on the website. People go down all the time. Just be careful. It's really slick and wet here."

She wasn't entirely sure she could do this, and stopped, shining her flashlight down when she was too afraid to tilt her head that far. Brett stood with her looking down.

"I don't know about this," he said.

"Unless we want to turn around and exit without finding what we came for, we have to keep going." It took all her strength to make her way down the slippery lava fall. At the bottom she fell on her rear and slipped the rest of the way.

Brett climbed down like a pro and landed on his feet. He thrust his hand out and helped her to stand again. Her legs shook, and she hoped he didn't notice. Kinsley didn't want to appear so incapable.

"Are you a rock climber or something?" she asked.

"Me? Nah. But I do a lot of hiking."

"Like where?"

"Mt. Rainier. Olympic National Park. That sort of thing. That's kind of how I ended up staying near Ruby Beach. I was planning a hike into the rainforest."

Wow. Okay. "And now you can't because you're helping me."

He shrugged and grinned. "The hike will be waiting for me on the other side of this."

By the looks of him, he did more than hiking. He wasn't hugely muscular, but he was still buff and strong. She shined her flashlight on the wall again and focused on the slime—about as far away as she could send her mind from how good Brett looked. If only she'd had one other person in the world she could have called to help.

He peered at the wall with her. "What are we looking for. I don't know if I would know it when I saw it."

"Think hockey puck. You know what that looks like, don't you? It's just a slice of silicon about that size, and it's covered in agar which is made from red algae or seaweed. It's a sweet substance to lure the microorganisms in. The bacteria needs to be able to make it through the membrane to the agar to be eligible for study. If it can't make it through, then it's no use when it comes to fighting viruses, bacteria or cancer."

"Thanks for the science lesson."

"You're welcome." She smiled to herself until they came on a rock formation that took up the entire tube. "How are we supposed to get around this?"

"We'll have to squeeze by or climb over and push through at the top."

"The information on the sign at the beginning of the cave said to follow this all the way to the exit, but I don't see how."

"It mentioned the rough spots. Come on, we can do it. But I have to say that it's hard to picture your boss going to all this trouble when we saw slime on the walls back there."

"Well, you don't know Max. He was a hobbyist caver before he was a microbiologist. He was all about caving, and he loved the fact that he could mix his love of caves with his science—it was like a dream job for him."

Until it wasn't. She refused to let those thoughts get her down. She was here for Max. To help find out what happened to him. To prevent what could happen to her.

She squeezed around the right space between the formation and the lava wall first, and she barely made it. "I don't know, Brett. You're broader than I am. If you get stuck, who's going to help us out?"

"I'll just suck in my breath." He made it through without much effort.

Was she fatter than she thought? She'd struggled more getting through. Before she could comment whispered voices drew their attention.

Then a gruff male voice said, "Come on, we need to catch them before it's too late. I got one more chance to get this done."

Oh, no. Fear spiked through her. She shared a look with Brett.

"I wish I had worn night vision goggles to get us out of this," he whispered.

"Next time." How could she tease at a time like this? "What are we going to do?"

"Take my hand." Brett's grip was strong as he led her deeper into the lava tube, then around another tube that branched off. "Now turn off the lights."

"And listen?"

"And keep quiet," he said so softly she barely heard.

But she could definitely hear her own breathing in the pitch-black quiet lava tube filled with millions of tiny creatures that could only be seen through a microscope. Kinsley shuddered at the thought—ridiculous considering she was a microbiologist.

Brett must have sensed her unease, though, and he wrapped his arm around her and pulled her in close. Why did he have to be so concerned and sensitive? So strong and comforting and caring and protective? His presence confused her mind and tugged at her heart.

While they shivered in the cold dark of the cave, hoping they wouldn't be found, Brett gripped his gun, hoping he wouldn't have to use it to protect her, but knowing he would do whatever he had to do. This wasn't the time or place to face off with anyone unless he was forced into it. He'd feared this exact scenario, while at the same time struggling to believe someone would actually come after them in the cave.

The Subaru guy had followed them but hadn't approached or attacked them. So was he just the information gathering part of this criminal operation?

Unfortunately, the light grew brighter along the tube that ran perpendicular to this one. Kinsley tugged on his hand and drew him deeper into an offshoot tube, using the dim setting on her flashlight to keep them from tumbling down another hole or lava fall. The deeper they went, the more concerned he was that they could get lost. He'd never imagined he could ever lose his way in a lava tube of all places.

When they couldn't see the light from the others anymore, Kinsley stopped and shined her light, illuminating the area—and then he saw what made her gasp. She pulled off her protective gloves and traded them for lab gloves.

Carefully she lifted the silicon mat and placed it into a Petri dish–like container, then into a specialized zippered cold-storage bag.

Shouts echoed down the tubes.

"Come on, we need to get out of here," he whispered.

"Wait, there's more. I need to get them all."

"No, you don't. We can come back for them."

But she'd bent over to retrieve the silicon wafers one at a time.

"There, I see a light." A male voice whispered.

Brett and Kinsley turned off their lights simultaneously. They'd given themselves away for microorganisms. He hoped it was worth it.

But there's no way we're making it out of here without light.

"Let's go." He shined his flashlight, trying to aim it away from where he'd last heard the voice, and they moved deeper into the lava tubes.

"I think we should get lost in here," she said.

"Get lost? I'm already lost, what are you talking about?"

"If we get lost, then they'll be lost too."

She had to be kidding. "What can you tell me about the lava tubes? Are we heading to a dead end?"

"How should I know? While I skimmed the information and saw there would be some rock piles, that's all the attention I paid to it. You know as much as I do. I'm just the girl who works in the lab. I didn't do any of this field-work with Max."

He exhaled. "Just wanted to make sure I'm not missing something. You have some samples so let's get out of here."

The sound of a couple of men climbing over a rock formation couldn't be missed. Brett flipped on the flashlight and then tugged her behind him. Just beyond the lava fall they met another few rock formations.

"I don't care that we're being chased, I want you to take your time getting over these. If you fall or twist an ankle or get injured, then we're going to be in a world of trouble."

As if they weren't already.

Why had the men suddenly decided to come for them in the cave? Had they been waiting for Kinsley to come here? Or had something happened to maybe speed up their timeline of following her? Had her accessing the data from the lab been the catalyst to send men after them today?

"Look, Brett. There's light up ahead."

They turned off their flashlights and headlamps.

"There's a hole in the ceiling. Can we get out through there?" She hoped so.

"No." He huffed. "No way we can make it."

NINE

With the light from the hole above shining in, they were exposed and needed to find a dark place to hide again.

She raced after Brett, who pulled her along as fast as they could travel down the treacherous path. Fear gripped her and she struggled to breathe. She would struggle to breathe at this pace even if she wasn't scared to death. Together they made their way through the rough cave environment as carefully as they could.

She was quickly regretting her decision to gather Max's specimens. Whatever he'd found would take time for her to sort through. Weeks or even months. She couldn't begin to hope to get answers they needed in a timely fashion.

In the end, this trip might have been a waste of time that only ended up putting them in danger. She saw that clearly now. Why couldn't she have come up with another way to find out who had blown up the lab?

But no, she'd insisted on going to the cave.

When they finally came to the metal ladder that would lead them out of the lava tube, she couldn't be more relieved. She raced for the ladder, but Brett turned and blocked her path.

Gripping her shoulders, he said, "We can't go up the ladder yet, remember?"

"Then what are we doing?" She couldn't wait to get out of here. Panic was causing her to lose her composure. She gulped for air.

"Breathe, Kinsley. Breathe. I'm going to protect you."

"What are we going to do?"

"I have an idea." He tugged her past the ladder into another portion of the cave and kept going until they discovered it was a dead end.

"This? This was your idea? This is the natural end of the lava tube. We're trapped. We should just take our chances on the ladder to the exit."

"Please calm down. Those guys are not going to get the best of us. We can't go up the ladder because I can't know if someone is waiting for us to come out."

"Like you said, you can't know. But we do know there are two men inside the cave looking for us and they're going to catch up."

"Those two guys are sent to flush us through the cave—but they wouldn't have come alone. I'm sure that others are waiting at the exit."

He held her gaze. Hoping she would figure out his plan? She drew in a few calming breaths. Closed her eyes and said a silent prayer.

"Okay. I'm calm and collected now. You hope if we hide here, those guys will go up the ladder and believe that we exited the cave."

"Exactly. Then we can go back the other way."

"No. We should wait. Chances are they'll backtrack and look for us in the parking lot. If someone was waiting outside when the two in the cave exit, they'll just head to the other exit, thinking we'll come out there."

"Then we can exit here? It might work— though there's still a chance they'll leave someone to guard the exit. You're right, though—it gives us fewer people to work around." His smile shouldn't make her feel so good inside.

"We'll just have to be flexible," she said.

"I like your thinking, Kinsley Langell." His words were breathy and his nearness did crazy things to her insides. Her heart. And her mind turned to mush when she was this close to him.

I once dreamed of being Kinsley Honor.
But you destroyed those dreams.
Just stop.

The two men after them made plenty of noise. Brett led her over to a wall, and she followed. Using his flashlight, he shined the beam on what looked like a pockmark in the lava. He gestured for her to get into the indentation. Though she didn't much like the idea of crawling into such a small spot, they were running out of time. The men would be on their heels soon and their only hope was to stay hidden until the danger passed. Inside the crevice, she pressed her back against the cold lava, which jabbed into her back even through the layers of her jacket. Brett stepped up and turned around, then pressed into the pockmark to join her, shielding her with his body. Then he turned off his flashlight.

And it was dark. So dark.

At least Brett's proximity kept her safe and, yes, warm. To get her back off the sharp and cold wall, she pressed forward into *Brett's* back. Not pushing him—he was too much a pillar for that—but she soaked up the reassurance his sturdy form provided.

God, please hide us in the shadow of your wings. Make us invisible so those bad guys will just walk right by.

She'd thought about trying to face them and get answers, but that was a bad idea. They'd simply have to wait until they discovered the truth—in a safe manner, if possible.

Voices sounded louder. The two men had made it to the ladder.

Go up the ladder. Go up the ladder. She

squeezed her eyes shut and tried not to let fear get the best of her.

"Hey, what if they went down here?" One of the men asked.

Oh, no. Why couldn't they just exit the cave? This was not good. Was not what they hoped for. Brett tensed in front of her. He probably held his gun ready to protect them too.

The darkness fled as someone shined a flashlight around.

"They aren't there. Look if you want, but it's a dead end. Don't be stupid."

"They could be hiding," the gravelly voice said.

Lord I can't take this. Please help us!

Light flooded the end of the lava tube. She feared what would come next. What would Brett do? She held her breath. Would he have to shoot someone to protect her? She wouldn't move or flinch, could barely even breathe, but instead she would wait for Brett to take action if necessary. She'd called him for a reason, and now she needed to trust him to do what he did best...

Save the day.

Brett's palm grew moist as he squeezed his pistol, ready to use it, though he hoped it wouldn't come to that.

As their follower shined his flashlight around

the end of the lava tube, Brett peeked from behind the edge of the pockmark, just a little. The man wasn't wearing a helmet with a headlamp. His face remained in the shadows, and Brett couldn't make it out.

The man studied the wall as though it might reveal a secret passage.

Come on, man, just move along.

The man turned the light along the wall where Brett and Kinsley were hidden. He pressed back against Kinsley, hoping they would not be discovered in the weirdly shaped indentation. But if they were, Brett was prepared to defend her with everything inside him.

The light moved over their hiding place and kept going. The man hadn't considered the shadow deep enough to hide them. Even so, Brett wouldn't let his guard down until they were out of this cave. Still shining the flashlight around as though he believed, or sensed, someone was in the lava tube where he searched, the man headed back out, finally passing their hiding place. Then he turned the corner and headed out of the end of the lava tube.

Brett listened to the steps grow distant. His shoulders sagged as he slowly released the breath he'd held. The ladder clinked and clanked—a relief to his ears—with a noise that sounded like two men climbing out. Kinsley pressed against Brett's back as if she expected him to step out of hiding, but he remained in place, and held his ground. Her idea about waiting for the men to leave and backtrack was a good one.

But not yet.

He didn't want to give up this spot until he was reasonably sure they were safe. He felt her warmth through his jacket, and the need to protect her ramped up a thousandfold. Though he wanted to wait a few more moments, he needed to see her and turned around to face her, finding himself entirely too close.

"Brett," she whispered, sounding breathless. Sounding like she felt for him, the way he felt for her.

No. This couldn't happen between them.

Shouting outside the exit echoed back down to them and he was both relieved for the distraction and the fact they hadn't made the mistake of taking that exit and stumbling into an ambush.

He didn't miss her slight gasp. Then, "you were right," she whispered. "Someone was waiting for us."

"Let's wait a little longer until it's quiet and then we can check and see if they're gone," he said.

Brett continued to press into the pockmark

and remain quiet. They couldn't leave their hiding place until he could be more certain it was safe.

Clanking sounds let him know the two men were coming back down the ladder. Uh-oh. What was happening?

"Sounds like they're backtracking," she said. "Going back through to try to flush us out that way. So that means those at this exit must be returning to the entrance."

"We can't know anything for certain." And that was a problem.

Either way, how long should they wait to make their move? After a couple more minutes ticked by, he eased away from Kinsley but pressed his finger to his lips. He leaned in to whisper.

"I'm going up that ladder to see if someone's still waiting."

"No, you can't," she said.

"I don't have a choice. Don't worry. I know how to handle myself."

"You want me to just wait here for you? What if the other two come back?"

"Follow me up the ladder but *wait* on the ladder. Once I've confirmed it's safe, then I'll let you know to come the rest of the way."

"And if the men come back through the cave?"

"It's going to take them some time to explore. They won't be back soon."

"What if we just follow them out and take the van out of here?"

"I think that option is off the table. I'm not spending any more time in this cave with those two. Let's get out of here, if it's safe." He stepped quietly forward.

Picked up a loose lava rock and held on. Then together they moved to the ladder. Brett braced himself for a battle, climbing quietly and gripping his gun and the rock, which wasn't easy.

Near the top, he threw the rock out. Any noise should draw out someone who was watching, alerting Brett to their presence.

After a few moments he heard only bird-song—a good sign they were alone.

Still...

Here goes nothing.

Brett inched his way slowly up and remained flat as he crouched on the ground crawling out the entrance, leading with his gun.

To his surprise, he could see no one was lurking in the underbrush or the woods. Still, they had to move fast because that could change at any moment. He looked down at Kinsley, who still waited on the ladder. "Come on. We need to hurry."

She climbed out and stood, then dusted off

her pants and secured her supply pack. "Now what? If we can't go back to the van, what are we going to do? We'll need to get another vehicle now that they know about that van."

Kinsley sighed. She was growing tired of this covert operation she'd been thrown into.

"Let's keep our voices down." He led her into the woods and off the main trail back to the entrance. "We can't take the trail since they're looking for us and waiting on us."

"Brett..."

"Don't worry. I'll get us out of this. You mentioned getting lost earlier. So we're going to get lost in the wilderness area surrounding the volcano."

"What?"

"Remember I said I hike. I know something about the area. I just haven't been in the caves."

He wasn't entirely sure either of them was up for a hike through the wilderness, but they both had packs—though their packs would have been much more robust if they'd known they'd need them for an actual hike through the wilderness that just might include an overnight stay.

He would contact Everly now, if he could, but there was no signal here in the dead zone. "I'll lead us through the woods until we find the two-lane road out of here." And that was another problem. The men after them knew that Brett and Kinsley weren't in the cave or their van, so that would mean they had to be following the road out. "There's only one and they'll take that road too, looking for us. That means we can't be seen walking anywhere near it."

"I have no choice but to trust you in this, Brett." She didn't sound happy about it.

He'd destroyed her trust before, and he didn't deserve a second chance with her, but at the very least he would like to make up for what he'd done in the past, and earn her trust back... for more than just protection

But what a way to have to do it.

TEN

Kinsley kept trying the burner cell phone, looking for bars, but this really was a wilderness area. No service. No connection. Even her GPS map wouldn't show up. She could see a dot on a grid, but that told her nothing. And her battery would soon die, considering the chargers were in the vehicle—not that there was anywhere she could have charged it.

"We should have gotten satellite phones," she said. If they'd known they would end up out in the middle of a dead zone, they could have gotten the phones. Then again, if they'd known they would end up here, they could have avoided it altogether. "Other than the time I spent with my parents overseas in underdeveloped areas, I've never been in a place where there was zero service. It's like the dead zone goes on forever."

Though it was spring, she was getting chilled as they hiked in the higher elevation. Fortunately, there wasn't any snow on the ground here at the moment—but that could change. Regardless, she would try not to whine or complain. She'd gotten them into this in the first place.

"Don't worry. We'll be out of here in no time." He slowed and turned to look at her and offered a smile, but his brows remained slightly furrowed.

She got the feeling he was trying to gauge if she was doing well with the hike. So far so good. But she would make no promises about the next hour or two or three. *Please, God, help us.*

He turned and continued leading her off-trail through the trees.

"Looks like most of the trees in this region are young, and have been recently replanted." She walked next to him between the trees.

He gave her a questioning look.

"I might not hike here, but I've read a lot about the area. After Max started going to the lava tubes, I was curious about the volcano."

"That's one of the reasons I enjoy hiking here. It's just so incredible to be able to look at a volcano that erupted only a few decades ago. I'll be honest—when I hiked here, I used the trails." He gave her a wry grin.

"I appreciate your honesty." *But I'm disappointed.* Still, she wouldn't whine.

"What else have you read about it?" he asked.

"Reforestation efforts have taken decades

and they still have tens of thousands of acres to plant. The eruption took out fifty-two thousand acres of trees."

He shook his head. "Can you imagine such power? That massive avalanche of melted rocks pushing down from the top of the mountains. All those trees being blown down or heated and killed. The animals and the fish decimated. Pyroclastic flows, mudflows."

"And now you can still see the ash along the riverbeds and streams and in the valley."

"Come on." His eyes brightened and he rushed through the trees and then suddenly stopped.

A steep ridge revealed a vast region still unplanted. And old dead tree trunks lay flat as if knocked down by a powerful force.

"There's the ash you were talking about, coloring everything a dusty silver color."

His hands were still gently gripping her, and for some insane reason, she didn't want him to let go. She smiled shyly at him and then stepped back.

"We should get going."

"Right." He led her back toward the direction they'd initially been heading.

She was glad to have broken that moment, still, it was nice having a conversation with him about something that interested them both and didn't include their past or more brainstorming to figure out who was behind Max's death. Regret filled her that she would take even one moment of solace before she learned the truth for him.

They continued for another half hour. They had gotten to the cave early in the morning. Glancing at the sun high in the sky, she figured it was around noon.

"How much farther before we make it to the road that can lead us out of the mountain area? Maybe we could hitch a ride."

He stopped and pulled his pack off. Sweat beaded at his temple. She wasn't sweating, but she was no longer cold, between the sun shining down on them and all the hiking.

He held her gaze briefly, then said, "We should hydrate."

Was he avoiding answering her question? She pulled off her pack and tugged out her water bottle and swirled it around. She didn't have much water left. They hadn't exactly prepped to go for a long hike through the wilderness. She took a sip of it and then closed it up.

Regret flashed in his eyes.

Because they were here? Because of their past? She wouldn't try to read his mind. She would just end up overthinking it.

He capped his bottle, then shifted on his feet, looking apologetic. "It's too risky to hitch a ride, even without someone chasing you. With what happened at the cave, my guess is there are at least four people involved in coming after you now. They're probably working for someone else—the person on the other end of the phone. I don't see that person as the kind of criminal that would get his hands dirty if he didn't have to, considering he hired others to blow up the lab. He would also hire them to come after you at the cave."

"You think there are two more in addition to the two outside of the lab, and Subaru guy. He could be one of them or not."

"In that case, possibly five. Regardless, it isn't safe to head for the road."

Kinsley's heart palpitated. Wait. "Are you saying this whole time we haven't even been walking toward the road?"

"We were for a while until I decided it simply isn't safe." Brett took a step toward her. One hand on his hip and the other palm out. "Listen, I won't sugarcoat it. This area is remote. We'll hike for a while longer, but we won't make it out before tonight, so we're going to need to make a camp before it gets dark."

Don't whine, don't complain. "What? Spend the night in the wilderness?" Kinsley tried not to hyperventilate. But she couldn't breathe.

Brett's brows furrowed. "I'm afraid so."

She calmed her breathing. Got control. Didn't think Brett noticed. "What if…what if we hike back to the cave and take our van? They can't still be waiting there. They must know we've gone."

"And they're hunting us. I don't know what their skill level is but the deeper we can go into the woods, the better. We can throw them off."

This is a worst-case scenario.

Not true. Getting blown up in a lab was the worst case and Max suffered that. Kinsley had it good in comparison and she should remember that. And she didn't want Brett to have to work harder at this than he already was.

"I'm sorry for giving you a hard time, especially since you're here helping me when you don't have to be. Let me know what I can do to help you."

A half smile rose on his lips and he stepped forward. "I'm glad I was here to help *you*, Kinsley. I had planned to be in Fiji, and…it's like… I don't know." He glanced off like he couldn't finish what he was going to say.

Like they were getting a second chance?

Oh, no. She wouldn't put herself through that again.

Kinsley resumed hiking. "I guess we'd better cover as much ground as possible and then stop to make camp. I'd love to get a signal and call for help, but then again, I'm in hiding. The person I would call is right here with me."

"It's going to be okay. I know about setting up a camp, even in the wilderness."

Even with killers hunting you?

Darkness would be on them sooner rather than later, and the temperatures would drop. Fortunately, they were headed to lower elevation, but the temps would still get down into the thirties or low forties. Though he didn't want to build a fire that could possibly give away their location, with the falling temps, they needed additional warmth. Unfortunately, they hadn't packed cold weather sleeping bags.

This scenario hadn't been in the realm of possibilities. So much for planning for all contingencies.

Maybe I made a mistake.

No. He'd made the only decision he could make—no one was going to find them out here. Unless, of course, they did. If anything, he'd made a mistake agreeing to visit the cave in the first place. Whoever was behind this was thinking of all eventualities of where Kinsley might go. They must have figured out that she was looking for the truth.

All this he thought through while he focused on building shelter for them to survive the night.

He found the right spot between two large trees the right width apart. Then he gathered wood to build a frame. Fortunately, he had a pocketknife, but it didn't help him all that much. He had to cut the pieces and then break them. While he worked to secure the frame, Kinsey gathered branches of a certain size that they could use to make the roof. Working together meant getting it done faster, plus it would take her mind off their predicament, and the movement would keep her warm.

She stacked the branches near him and glanced up at him. She smiled, but he could see behind her smile that she wasn't happy. Was she angry with him? He couldn't think about that right now.

"Thanks. You did good."

"Now what?" she asked.

"We stack the branches like this." He showed her how to lean them together and create a roof, sort of.

"I've seen lean-tos before. I guess this is our only choice for shelter."

"That's right. If you can finish stacking the branches, then I'll work on the fire. The lean-to will catch the heat from the fire and keep us warmer."

"Were you a Boy Scout or something?"

He looked at her but said nothing as he gathered kindling.

"I'm only teasing. You were in the military—I haven't forgotten."

Kindling and wood arranged, he used the fire starter from his pack. Strange to think that had been included but not sleeping bags or a tent.

The fire blazed to life, and he breathed a sigh of relief. He glanced over his shoulder as Kinsley approached. The lean-to was ready. He just needed to put some pine needles down to soften the ground.

Kinsley sat on the bigger log he'd arranged and pulled her gloves off to rub her hands. "You make a mean survival camp, Brett."

This time her smile came through in her eyes.

"I'm sorry I can't make you more comfortable, Kinsley."

"Oh, come on, Brett. We couldn't have known this would happen."

He frowned. "Maybe we should have prepared for the possibility, because here we are."

"Yes, here we are, and you *are* prepared for this possibility. We have shelter and a little water. Some protein bars and a couple of blankets. We'll be fine, and that's thanks to you." She squeezed his shoulder.

He enjoyed the feel of her touch a little too much.

"If anyone should apologize, it's me," she

added. "I shouldn't have insisted the cave was a good idea."

"If I was as prepared as I should have been, I'd have brought more items in our packs," Brett argued back, uncomfortable with the way she was praising him. "We would have it a lot better tonight. Be comfy in warm sleeping bags."

"Well, there's enough blame to go around so we won't waste any more time talking about it. I'll just say that with all our modern technology and satellites, it seems ridiculous to have a dead zone. Remind me to buy a satellite phone once we're out of this. I never want to be stranded in a dead zone again."

"Yeah, except you will probably never again have a need for one."

She huffed a laugh. "I'm not a wilderness girl, but—" she lifted her shoulders, then angled her hand "—I'm trying to keep an open mind."

Then she looked at him.

Chills ran over him. Not the bad kind. The good kind. Was she saying what he thought she was saying? That she might want to go hiking with him sometime? Nah, she couldn't be saying that. He wasn't thinking right.

And if she was saying that, he was giving her the wrong vibes. Once she was safe, he'd be out of her life again. This time for good.

She hugged herself and rubbed her arms.

"Still cold?" he asked.

"Yep and hungry. Are you going to hunt our dinner or dig for roots or scavenge for nuts and berries?"

That set off a full-on laugh before Brett caught himself. He didn't need to draw any more attention than he already had by building a fire. Sounds traveled a long distance out there. He hoped and prayed those men had stuck to the road and other obvious places to search for them.

"That's okay. I'll cook dinner," she said and picked up her pack. She pulled out the protein bars and tossed him one. "After all, you made a fire and everything."

"Don't sell yourself short. You helped build the lean-to."

They ate in silence for a few moments, and Brett waited until he'd finished the entire bar before he sipped on his water. That was another thing he should have packed—more water, or a way to purify water. They had enough for another day's hike if they were careful, but that was the worst-case scenario. He hoped they were out of the woods sometime early tomorrow.

"Can we get in the lean-to now?"

"I think that's a good idea. The fire and our… um…proximity…will keep us warm. We'll be fine."

God, please let us be fine.

Her eyes widened. "You mean…"

He couldn't help his smile. "Don't look so horrified. I'm not that bad, am I?"

Oh, yes, he was. He'd hurt them both. And while he'd withdrawn from her to spare her from more pain, he knew the end of their relationship couldn't have been easy on her. Maybe tonight he needed to tell her everything. Explain everything to her.

For what purpose, though? Telling her why he'd broken off with her would make an already intolerable situation even more unbearable. But with the thoughts, Brett realized that he was carrying the burden of that breakup around with him. He needed to tell her—to get that guilt off his chest. But would he only be hurting her all over again?

Hurting them both?

Maybe he should just leave it in the past and focus on the very real and present danger.

"You're not that bad." She smiled. "Besides, desperate times call for desperate measures, right?"

Right, because you could only be desperate to snuggle with me, that's for sure.

ELEVEN

Kinsley wished she hadn't said those words. She'd only been teasing. She certainly wouldn't have to be desperate to snuggle with Brett under any circumstances. Still, she felt a little awkward.

But she was cold, and they needed to stay warm. They both gathered needles and leaves, and for good measure, Brett positioned a log so they'd have something to lean against.

"Would you prefer I leave the log out and we can just lie here instead?"

"The log is good for now and we can watch the fire for a while."

"I have a feeling we're both going to fall asleep from sheer exhaustion."

"You might be right."

"And once I sit down, I don't think I'm going to get back up soon." He quirked a grin, but she saw the exhaustion on his face and in the set of his shoulders.

"Let's leave the log." It was better to ease into this situation. Lying down together felt too intimate. She crawled into the lean-to and sat on the soft ground, then leaned against the log. He followed her in and wrapped his arm around her for warmth. She snuggled against him and stared at the fire. Back when they were a couple, they'd never actually been camping. She hadn't known he'd enjoyed hiking, even. Was that something new or had he always been more of an outdoorsman? She thought she'd known him—she'd loved him—but then again even when someone knew someone well, it could take a lifetime to learn everything. And she'd wanted that lifetime with him.

Back then.

She shouldn't think about what they'd had together before because that did her no good now—but being here made it difficult not to wonder. He remained tender and caring and all-around good in every way and it baffled her that he wasn't already married. Didn't have a girlfriend.

Wait a minute. Maybe he *did* at least have a significant other, but she'd failed to ask and he'd failed to tell her. For that matter, maybe she hadn't asked because she was afraid of the answer, which seemed crazy. But no way would she ask him now, while she was curled up in his arms. Besides, he wouldn't have been staying on the beach alone if he was married.

Okay. Good. She could stop worrying. Smiling to herself, she relaxed into him. Warmth infused her. She could let herself fall asleep just like this. Unfortunately, that meant she might be getting entirely too comfortable against him.

Being with him felt far too good, and right.

This is completely surreal.

She couldn't have imagined this moment in her wildest dreams. At least they weren't snuggling out of affection for each other. Instead they were just trying to survive. How could her life have come to this moment where she was cuddling with the man she used to love— a man who'd broken her heart—in order to live through the night and not freeze to death?"

A log fell and startled her from her sleepy thoughts. "The fire's going out. Will we be okay?"

"I'll need to stoke it, but I won't add more firewood. Not yet. My guess is the temperature is around 40 and will only go lower tonight. We'll have to be careful not to run through our fuel too fast. We don't want to get hypothermia." He pulled her closer.

The comfort of the gesture felt like much more than survival or desperation.

It felt…personal.

"Don't worry. We'll survive," he said as if reading her mind.

Will we? She chewed on her lips—to keep them from chattering, but she wasn't really cold so her chattering was more from fear and anxiety.

Brett suddenly extracted himself from her. "I need to check around to make sure no one has followed us. I'll stoke the fire while I'm at it."

She instantly felt colder as he crawled from the lean-to and pulled out his gun. The sight of his handgun reminded her of their precarious situation.

"We know they'll be waiting and watching for us to show up somewhere," she stated. "But do you really think they're out here in the cold searching? Because if we got lost out here to avoid them for nothing, I'm going to be upset." Kinsley forced a smile. But really, what was the point of suffering through the cold if those men found them here anyway?

"I'm just trying to be cautious."

She hugged herself. "*I'll* stoke the fire. Please don't be long."

"I won't. Stay here. I'll check around and then be back soon to stoke the fire. You just stay in the lean-to and stay warm. No sense in two of us getting up."

"I can help."

He crouched back in and kissed her forehead. "I know you can. And you will. We're going to figure out who is behind this."

He stood tall and chambered a round in his gun. The sound sent fear crawling over her.

Then he slipped away into the night and Kinsley curled into herself. When he'd leaned back in, she hadn't known what to expect and, for a split second, she thought he might kiss her, and that would have surprised her. She felt the tenderness of even a peck on the forehead. He cared...he still cared in a personal way. But Kinsley could not let that break down the barriers around her heart. They were here in this situation together to survive. She owed him for his help, for his protection, but at the same time, she needed to protect her heart.

A twig snapped nearby.

Kinsley stiffened.

Sat up.

Brett?

Unease crawled over her, and she gave up the warmth she'd settled into and scrambled out of the lean-to. The fire was dwindling but still produced a ring of light that prevented her from seeing into the darkness. She moved to the fire and kicked dirt into it to extinguish it, then spread the last embers around so it wouldn't lead anyone to them. Brett could always rebuild it, but they had to survive for that to happen.

She moved away from their rudimentary camp to stand behind a tree in the darkest shadows. Waited and listened. But she couldn't hear anything over her own heart pounding.

Brett, please come back.

Kinsley crouched to pick up a branch. She needed something to use as a weapon. Brett had the gun, after all.

Voices...whispers...sounded, and she held her breath.

They were too close if she could hear their whispers.

What had happened to Brett?

"Looks like they were here," a familiar voice said.

It was the same guy at the lab who'd spoken with someone on the phone. One of the same creeps who'd followed them through the lava tube.

"It could have been anyone here. We don't know if it was them. We've lost them. Give it up," a second man growled.

"I'm not calling in until we've finished this business."

"Remember. Whatever we do, it's going to have to look like an accident."

"The police are looking for her. They think

she caused the explosion. We just have her commit suicide."

"We have to find her first before it's too late."

Kinsley listened as she held her breath. If they found her here, it would all be over. She couldn't move. She couldn't breathe.

God, please help me.

"Let's go. I'm done searching these woods. It's too cold out here."

"They'll show up sooner or later."

"You'd better hope sooner, for our sakes."

She heard a few more rustling sounds that got farther away—like the men were leaving. She hoped they wouldn't take a turn that would make them accidentally stumble on her.

A hand covered her mouth and she started to fight back, but he whispered in her ear. "It's me."

She relaxed against Brett. He had come back, and he'd probably heard them as well. But he'd risked drawing their attention with his movements to get to her.

"They're gone. But we'll wait here for a little longer," he whispered again.

His breath was soft and warm against her cheek.

She'd been terrified, but his presence chased the fear away. How did he do that?

"You ready?" He stepped away from her.

"Is it safe to stay here?"

"I think so. But I need to wait for a while before I build a fire again. Okay?"

Brett had never been so happy to see dawn. Still, the early morning brought the lowest temperatures and he felt stone-cold, even with Kinsley in his arms. Holding her, protecting her all night, he hadn't slept a wink. How could he?

He spent the entire night listening for their stalkers to return. Just like Brett had waited for the men to move on, they could have simply been waiting for Brett and Kinsley to return to their camp. Honestly, since they'd left their packs right there in the camp, he was surprised the men hadn't figured out it was, in fact, their prey that had been camping there. Maybe they'd just been waiting to ambush Brett and Kinsley while they slept.

Hence, he couldn't sleep. Military training had taught him how to run on fumes, but it didn't help his physical state that it was so cold. When they needed warmth from the fire the most—the coldest hours of the night—it had died.

Kinsley was still asleep, and he hated to risk waking her, hoping to give her a few more moments of rest. He carefully disentangled himself from her and repositioned her head on the soft warm leaves. Good. She hadn't woken up.

He noted how peacefully she slept despite the rough night, and how beautiful she was while sleeping.

He crawled from the lean-to and was hit with significantly colder air. He'd only *thought* it was cold inside his rudimentary shelter. Gun ready, he glanced around them for any possible threat before he stoked the fire to get it going again and keep Kinsley warm.

He had to admit he was impressed with her. She worked in a lab all day every day and wasn't accustomed to hiking in the wilderness, much less in such stressful circumstances. The strain had to be taking a toll, but she was a trooper and had kept up with him without complaint. He already admired her, but that admiration grew to a whole new level during this experience. And did nothing to help him rein in his emotions where she was concerned.

He hadn't been able to shake the warm feelings flooding him. The desire to protect her, keep her safe and warm for the rest of his life ignited in his heart again. He had absolutely no business entertaining those kinds of thoughts.

Dreams.

He admitted that another reason he hadn't fallen asleep last night with her in his arms was because he was still having nightmares, and he often woke himself up in violent way. He usually punched the bed or the wall. Ayden was right—he needed to get his head together and maybe consider seeing a therapist.

Again.

But all of that meant he could just push away any thoughts of second chances with Kinsley. He was a danger to her in more than one sense. He was supposed to protect her, and that was what he meant to do—that, and nothing more. Surely he could work through this with Kinsley and keep matters of the heart out of it.

Or at least at bay.

Crouching near the fire, he wished he could make coffee, but he had no grounds to go with the remaining water. At least he had a few more granola bars. This would have to see them through until they were out of the literal woods.

She stirred and sat up, rubbed her eyes. Her bobbed brown hair fell across her face and he wanted to gently brush it away.

"Good morning, sleepyhead."

"What time is it?" She yawned.

"My cell phone and smartwatch both died. But looking at the sky, I'd say it's probably around half past morning."

"It's freezing."

"I know. The fire's going if you want to move closer. We can have breakfast and then get moving."

She crawled over and sat next to him on the log. He handed her a bottle of water and a protein bar.

"Thanks. I'm so hungry that I was dreaming about food." She laughed.

"Oh, yeah? What kind?"

"All kinds. I dreamed of eating a big juicy cheeseburger and large fries. The most amazing roast beef that my mom used to make years ago." She tore into the bar.

"You're a twig. You don't eat like that."

"Not all the time, but when I'm hungry, sure."

"Then first thing we do when we're out of this wilderness is grab burgers and fries." At the mention of burgers and fries, his stomach rumbled. He couldn't eat more bars, they had to ration them just in case they didn't make it out of here today like he hoped and planned.

"That sounds good. Maybe we can celebrate when this nightmare is over."

Yeah…but when this nightmare was over, they would go their separate ways. Still, maybe one last celebratory meal of cheeseburgers and fries wouldn't hurt.

"Sounds like a plan. And this nightmare will end soon, Kinsley. Don't worry. We'll find out who killed Max."

"And who wants to kill me?" she said. "You heard them talking last night, didn't you?"

"Yes." He'd hated that she'd heard them too. "Did you see them?"

"I couldn't get a good look in the dark, and I didn't want to give my presence away by *trying* to see them. At least Everly is running the Subaru license plate. Hopefully, that will tell us something." Even smart criminals sometimes made mistakes like using a vehicle that could tie them to a crime. But Everly couldn't tell them anything until they could communicate.

Kinsley finished her protein bar and dusted off her hands. She folded up the blanket they'd used and stuffed it back in his pack.

"I'm ready to go when you are."

He put out the fire and covered it with rocks and dirt. They set out again. She favored her right foot, and he suspected her feet were probably blistered by now. Without the right kind of shoes and socks for hiking, blisters were hard to avoid. He should have inspected her feet last night. There was a small First Aid kit in his pack. If they didn't get out of here soon, he'd have to address that.

To her credit, she said nothing, but now and then he caught a pained expression on her face.

"Something we need to think about is that they could come back to find us during the day. They can see us with binoculars or fly over with a helicopter," Brett pointed out.

"So if we hear a helicopter we aren't going to wave at them because we need rescuing?"

"I don't think we can risk it."

"How are we going to get out of this, Brett?"

He pointed to the mountainside. "There's the road. Today we're following the road from a distance, and we'll head into the valley, sticking close to the tree line. We hear a helicopter, then we take cover in the trees."

"Are we going to call someone when I get cell service? I mean, you can't, because your cell and watch are dead. I turned mine off last night."

She'd been smart and turned it off to save what was left of her battery. "Well, who would you like me to call?"

"I get your point."

I was hoping you would tell me to bring in Honor Protection Specialists. But he wouldn't push her. Not yet. Although they were reaching the breaking point.

"Brett, I see something down there. Looks like we're getting close to civilization. I'm going to turn my phone on."

"I still have no bars." She frowned. "But maybe they can help us."

"It looks like a small airstrip." He scrutinized the spread before him.

"What? I don't see anything. Where?"

"It's a grass airstrip. And see what looks like a big red barn?" Brett pointed. "That's a hangar."

"Wow, do you think they're home?"

"I hope so," he said. "I have an idea."

"You're going to ask him to fly us out of here?"

"Maybe."

She drew in a quick breath. "But Brett, look. There's a car turning in, driving up to that place."

"I see it." *The Subaru.*

That could ruin his plans to secure a safe route out of the wilderness. Was the man driving the Subaru with the police? Was he canvassing the areas and warning people to be on the lookout for Brett and Kinsley, asking people to call the police? Given how openly he was acting, Subaru guy had to be PD or connected somehow. No doubt about it. And there was no doubt Brett was now on their radar. It wasn't safe for Subaru man to see either one of them.

"What are we going to do now?" she asked. She kept her tone even and strong, but she couldn't hide the exhaustion along with a hint of discouragement.

Brett grabbed her hand and squeezed. She looked up at him and then he saw just how much she was depending on him, trusting him. He wasn't sure that was such a good idea because both their hearts were on the line.

"We confront the problem. Fight. Win."

"I think you stole that line from *The Incredibles*."

He smiled. "What can I say? I had to spend some time recently with a twelve-year-old client. We watched a lot of movies, played some basketball and read classics. What's your excuse for recognizing it?"

At her suddenly sad expression, he kind of wished he hadn't asked.

She started hiking toward the valley with the airstrip as the Subaru pulled out and drove away. "What can I say? I spend a lot of time *alone* watching movies."

TWELVE

She laughed and shrugged to hide her embarrassment. How could she have said that out loud?

Could I be any more pathetic?

And when Brett said nothing in response, the awkwardness she felt only grew.

But she didn't have to share the details of her boring life with him, especially since she now knew she wanted to make a change. Being with him opened her eyes to what she had been missing in life. Really, she had only been existing, not actually living. But now wasn't the time to think about the bigger issues of what she wanted out of life. She needed to focus on living to see another day.

Or even another hour.

The hike down the ridge through the new tree growth to the valley below had taken over an hour. Kinsley stood tall and held her chin high so Brett wouldn't worry about her, but when he glanced at her, she had a feeling he saw right through her.

Remaining in the shadows of the trees at the edge of the farm/private airstrip, he stopped and looked around.

"Why are we stopping?" she asked. "What are you thinking?"

"I'm thinking it might be better if you stay here in the shadows while I go check this place's owner out and ask for help. After all, who knows what Subaru guy told him. Approaching anyone is risky. They could try to keep us there and turn us in."

"No way. I'm not standing out here alone, so don't even think about leaving me behind." She pressed her cold hands on her hips.

Brett sighed. "If we walk across the airstrips, whoever lives here is going to see us and call someone before I can even talk to him."

"Then we just move past this opportunity of help and find someone else. We go to the next place, plane or no plane. Subaru guy ruined this for us."

"That's just it—he could be canvassing this entire valley, knowing this is our shortest route from the wilderness area. Anyone we talk to now is going to be risky."

"What should we do?"

He rubbed his jaw. "Let's edge around the

barn. Maybe the owner won't see us in time to call the police before we get a chance to plead our case."

"And you really think the owner is going to listen to you?"

"We have to try. Or we can keep walking."

"I would say we could finally call for help, but my phone has now finally died." She growled. "Why didn't I turn it off, Brett?"

"You were waiting on the bars." He turned to her and gently pressed his hand on her shoulders. "We're both exhausted. We hadn't planned to hike the volcano wilderness or spend the night, but we're here now. Do you want to keep hiking?"

She sighed. "No. Let's visit whoever's here first and see what happens. Lead on."

They continued around the edges of the woods and then walked forward at the back of the barn.

"I'm not going to make an attempt to try to hide our presence here because if we're caught, our actions will go against our credibility. At the same time, I don't want to draw any attention until the last possible moment."

Finally at the door, Brett rang the doorbell. Once they'd gotten closer, Kinsley hadn't missed the cameras. A guy opened the door. He helda cell phone at his earand a gun at his side.

Oh, no. Had he already made the call to the police? Kinsley sagged. Brett had put his gun away for which she was grateful. They needed to win this guy over if it wasn't too late.

Kinsley hoped they weren't making a mistake.

Brett spoke up, holding his hands halfway to show he meant no harm. "I apologize for the intrusion, but we got lost in the wilderness region and we need help. Our cell phones have died" And were worthless, even if they hadn't been in a dead zone.

The man pressed his lips into a flat line. "I received a visit from someone warning me about two dangerous people, instructing me to call him if I saw you."

Brett glanced at the cell phone. "And you already called him."

"No." The man opened the door wider and glanced around outside behind them as he gestured them inside, then shut the door.

Brett looked at Kinsley. To reassure her? "Why…why didn't you call him?" she asked. Oops. Maybe Brett had wanted her to let him do the talking."

"I'll explain." He put his gun away. "Come in out of the cold."

Kinsley followed Brett inside the warm and cozy house.

"You look like you've had a rough day," the older man said. "Have a seat. I'll get you water. Are you hungry?"

"Water's good to start. But you haven't told us why you didn't call him—or just call 911. You haven't heard our story yet either."

"I heard one story, though maybe it isn't the true one. Time enough to hear your take. My name's Gil, by the way."

Kinsley shared a look with Brett. Were they telling him their names?

"I saw your picture on the news, I know who you are."

Brett's eyes grew wide. So he was in the news now too, since he'd been identified helping Kinsley. His siblings were probably furious. Kinsley might have no choice but to trust them to help, but she would wait for Brett to make that call.

After hydrating and resting her sore feet, she let Brett explain their predicament.

"I knew that guy was up to no good," Gil said. "His name was Lee Jackson. Showed me ID and claims he's working with the police to locate two fugitives."

Fugitives? Panic spiked through her chest. This just got better and better.

"Why didn't you believe him?" Brett's tone was a little suspicious if not incredulous.

"He was cagey, and something felt off." Gil

looked at Brett. "I saw you're a vet. Former army. A helicopter pilot. I was a marine, and my son followed in my footsteps, but he was killed in Afghanistan. So I want to help you any way I can. Now that I've talked to you, I know you're being falsely accused."

Kinsley swelled with pride and admiration for Brett. "Thank you both for your service and your sacrifice," she said. "Brett and I met when he rescued me and my family from a flood. They worked with Doctors Without Borders."

Gil smiled. "I knew I liked you two."

Oh, why did she have to bring up when she and Brett had met? *What am I doing? Time to redirect.* Something caught her eye, and even though it wasn't connected to their current situation, she latched onto it. "I see you have a lot of photos of Mt. St. Helens, before and after."

"I lived here in this valley for ten years before the eruption," he said. "I loved to hike with my boys and took a lot of pictures. This place was far enough away we didn't get flattened, but we evacuated just the same. From a safe distance, I took as many pictures as I could until there was nothing to see but an ash-filled sky. I have a couple of thick albums on the shelf."

He stood and she thought he would to grab the albums to show her but instead he moved to the kitchen, which was only separated from the

living room by a wide counter. "I've been sim-
mering chili all day. You want some? If you do,
you'll have to be quick. I don't think you have
a lot of time. Jackson could return at any time.
He said he was canvassing the area and talking
to people, but I spoke to my neighbors on each
side, and he didn't visit them."

Gil leveled his gaze on Brett, who nodded
slowly and then spoke.

"You think he targeted you because he thinks
I'm coming for one of your planes."

"That would be my guess." Gil dipped up
bowls of chili as if he expected them to eat. He
pushed the dishes forward, then grabbed spoons
and a package of crackers. "Eat up while it's
hot and while you still can. You probably need
the energy and the warmth. The way you two
look, it might take all day to get that chill out
of your bones."

"Thanks." Kinsley moved to the counter and
eagerly dug into the chili.

Brett joined her. "How can we thank you?."

"You can thank me by getting out of here
safely and making this right. Let justice pre-
vail. For my part, I have one of two planes you
could use to get out of here."

Brett's eyes brightened. "Are you sure? I don't
want to put you out."

"Please, put me out. I want to help." Gil

squeezed Brett's shoulders like he was a long-lost father.

Tears emerged in Kinsley's eyes—maybe it was from the exhaustion of the day, but the moment was somehow poignant.

"I'm grateful I have this opportunity to help," Gil said. "Take whatever you need. More water, food or supplies. In addition to the communication in the plane, I have a mobile radio and satellite phone that you can take with you, and a few other things you might need."

"Gil, I really don't know what to say." Brett cleared his throat. "Thank you doesn't seem like enough. I really insist on repaying you somehow for your generosity. What can I do to repay you?"

Gil's grin was toothy. "Try to return my plane in one piece after this is over. That's all I ask."

Kinsley and Brett quickly finished off their chili. If she was honest, she wanted another bowl, but they had to leave before that opportunity passed and they were caught. Kinsley took their bowls to the sink and washed them out. Then she approached Gil. She couldn't help herself, and hugged this stranger who was a life raft to them. He had a strong grip and patted her on the back. "You're going to be okay. You just hang in there and the truth will come out."

An alarm sounded on Gil's phone. He reached

for it, checking the screen with a frown. "Looks like we've got company. Jackson is coming back for you just like I suspected he would."

Gil gestured toward a door. "Let's get you out of here. Follow me."

He kicked into gear, moving surprisingly fast for a man his age.

Brett pulled Kinsley along with him as they followed Gil. At a side door and mudroom, Gil lifted a pack off a shelf and tossed it to Brett. "That gear I mentioned. This is my emergency to-go bag. Already preppedfor any contingency."

Brett and Kinsley followed Gil through the door and across an asphalt walkway to the big red hangar that looked like a barn. Unlocking the barn doors, he pulled them wide open and urged them inside.

A red and white Cessna 172 sat in the space next to a blue Piper Cherokee. Nice.

Gil gestured to the Cessna. "She's ready to take out. I did a preflight check a couple of hours ago and was out to take off when I was interrupted. You have blue skies and good weather. Feel free to do your own. I'll try to hold off Jackson, but I can't guarantee he won't barge right in here."

"I can't thank you enough."

"Like I said, you can thank me by staying safe and alive. Go on. I'll put him off as long as I can." Gil looked at Brett, respect in his eyes, and then nodded at both Brett and Kinsley, and smiled as though pleased he could be part of this covert operation.

He turned and left them in the barn.

Brett opened the plane's door and tossed the pack in the back. He and Kinsley tossed the packs they'd brought with them in the back as well.

Kinsley climbed into the passenger seat and buckled in, and Brett got comfortable in the captain's chair in the cockpit. Put on his headset and handed one to Kinsley. This had worked out better than he could have imagined.

He couldn't help but smile even though they weren't out of danger yet. He turned his smile on Kinsley as he started up the plane. "Let's get out of here."

"Are you sure it's a good idea to leave Gil to Jackson alone?"

"He can handle himself, and he's giving us a chance to escape. Lee Jackson, if that's his real name, has followed us and never attacked us. Whoever's paying him, I doubt they want the bad publicity of attacking a senior citizen vet who's also a gold star parent. We're getting out of here." The biggest issue was timing. He would love for Jackson to be inside the house or out of the way as Brett taxied down the runway.

Brett familiarized himself with the Cessna once again, then slowly taxied out of the hangar and onto the smooth grass of the airstrip. If he ever moved to the country, he was definitely putting one of these in. Brett increased speed and prepared to lift off as soon as he could. Unfortunately, he spotted Gil and Jackson at his front door, arguing. Jackson suddenly turned and spotted the plane. He rushed toward his Subaru.

"What are we going to do?"

"We're going to get in the air and he's not going to stop us."

While Brett worked to increase speed so he could fly away, in his peripheral vision he watched Gil chase after Jackson, who turned and aimed his gun. Gil dove behind a tree. Kinsley screamed. "Brett, we can't leave Gil."

"And neither can we stay."

At least Jackson wasn't going after Gil anymore. The Subaru peeled through the grass and increased speed as if Jackson intended to block Brett's path. Kinsley tensed next to him.

"Just hold on. We're going to make it."

Accelerating, he gritted his teeth as if that would somehow get them in the air. The Subaru parked right in his path as he pulled back the yoke to lift the plane.

Come on, come on come on...

The Cessna flew straight over the car, missing it by inches. Brett released a heavy exhale and took satisfaction in watching Lee Jackson duck as they flew over. But bullets pinged the fuselage before the plane was out of range.

"He shot at us, Brett," Kinsley said, sounding shaky. "Now you'll have to return Gil's plane with bullet holes."

"The guy might actually appreciate them as battle scars." He banked right to fly back over the farm and check on Gil.

The Subaru was speeding away and Gil waved at them. Brett waved back and then headed north. "Look, Gil's okay. Jackson didn't hit him. I hope Gil calls the police to let them know. But then again he could get the dirty cop on that call."

"Gil's sharp. He'll know how to handle it. He's given us a chance and we're not going to let him down."

"Fair enough. If you're sure he's all right, then I won't worry about him too much, but where are we going?" Kinsley asked.

Good question. "I need you to retrieve that satellite phone if you can. I don't have a flight plan." He turned off the transponder so no one could track them but he was flying illegally. The faster he could land, the better."

"Here, found the phone."

"Now, punch in the number I give you, and let me talk to Everly." Brett spared a glance at Kinsley. "This plane is compromised. Jackson will get hold of the police, and they're going to track us and arrest us where we land. So we need to land and get away from the plane. If Jackson hadn't returned, it would be a different story."

Everly answered. "Everly Honor speaking."

"Everly, it's Brett."

"Brett. I've been so worried about you. What in the world is going on? I saw you on the news. Of course, Ayden and Caine saw you too. I haven't told them anything yet, but I can't hold out much longer. You have to bring them in on this officially, Brett."

Once again Brett glanced at Kinsley. He wanted to earn her trust. He wouldn't betray it. "Not yet, Everly. Not yet. Look, if they press you, just tell them they need to trust me. When the time is right, then we can bring them in. Until then, the less they know, the better."

"And what about me?" Everly asked.

"Well, you're in it now whether you like it or not."

"How am I supposed to work with you and help you and hide it from them?"

"You'll figure it out. Ask them to trust you. They owe you that much. You've trusted them to keep their clients' secrets at times."

"Ayden isn't going to be happy about this."

"Sounds like you're just working up the courage to face him."

"Maybe I am." A heavy sigh came over the phone. "What exactly do you need from me?"

"We need a safe house. Off-grid. But we still need to be able to connect to the world to do our research. Not many people can arrange that. I'm glad you're one of those who can."

"Can you at least tell me what's going on?"

He glanced at Kinsley. She pursed her lips but slowly nodded. "Yeah. I have the go-ahead."

Brett explained the predicament concisely and Kinsley added a few more details.

"I see," Every said. "While you've been talking, I've been searching. I'm going to set you up with a house, but that will take some time. I can help you figure this out too, now that you've read me in. In the meantime, let me look at the map. Where are you?"

He gave her the GPS location.

"Hold on. I'm looking. Okay… You can set that plane down along a dirt farm road if you head east. It's out in the middle of nowhere."

"We don't need middle of nowhere. Been there, done that."

"Ha. I get it, after how you spent last night. But don't worry—you'll definitely have a roof over your head this time. I'll also tell Gil where he can pick up his plane and arrange payment for his assistance. I have a contact who will transport you. I can't be seen coming for you... depending on how deep this goes. Someone could follow me."

"Someone else involved?" Kinsley glared at Brett. "It's too risky."

"Everly?" She'd said nothing in response to Kinsey's question. He wasn't sure she was still there.

"I'm here. Try to land at the corner of Farm Road 1243 and Statin Drive. Walk a mile down that farm road and the car will be waiting, hidden in the trees. I'll have it dropped off in advance—no one will be there to see you. The fob will be in the wheel rim."

Brett glanced at Kinsley again, hoping she was still on board. She'd asked him to help her, but she hadn't hired him to run a protection detail, so he wouldn't bulldoze over her to do things his way. He wanted to earn her trust in the worst way. Or maybe it was the best way.

"Okay, that sounds like a plan," he said.

"Contact me again later and I'll have the information on the nearest safe house. I'm on it, Brett. You can count on me."

"I know I can. Thanks, sis." *What would I do without you?*

Kinsley ended the call for him.

Brett looked at the dashboard and noticed the fuel tank was almost empty. He glanced out the window. One of those bullets had hit the gas tank.

THIRTEEN

"What's wrong?" Kinsley hadn't missed the way Brett's features had tightened.

"Nothing."

"Don't give me that. I know you." Bother. Why did she keep having to refer to their shared past? She'd prefer to forget it.

"Okay. Look," he said. "One of the bullets must have knocked a hole in the gas tank. We should have had enough gas for a few hours of flying time, but now it's almost empty."

"Oh, no, Brett. What are we going to do?" How could she survive an explosion and men after her, only to die in a plane crash.

I don't want to die!

"Relax, Kinsley. Breathe. I can land this. We have plenty of glide time before we need to land. I know what I'm doing. This wouldn't be the first time I've had to glide to a landing." But images of the helicopter crash accosted him.

Not now. He growled inside.

"Then why do you have that look on your face?"

"Come on. It's easy to guess that I have more control when the engine has fuel, and I have the power. Now I'm relying on the forces of nature."

"The forces of nature?"

"You're a scientist so I'm sure that makes sense. In my world as a pilot, four forces of nature are manipulated to allow for flight—lift, weight, drag and thrust. I don't have power to increase speed which is what's needed to get lift, but I still have enough to work with."

"Okay, Brett. I trust you."

I trust you.

Had she really just said that to him? This time when she said it, the words pinged through her heart as though she'd meant something deeper, something more than she trusted him to simply protect her through this.

But that couldn't be true. She didn't trust him beyond this fight for justice and survival.

And she trusted him to land. With that, Kinsley calmed her breathing and stared out the window at the mountains to the west and the farmland and small town, rivers and woods beneath them. *God, why am I here? What is going on?*

All she and her family had ever wanted to do was help others, and her parents had died senselessly. Her sister too. And now Max, her last connection to her family was dead. Murdered. And Kinsley's work had all turned to ash. They had been trying to save people. Who could possibly have something against helping the world through new drug discoveries?

"We're approaching the farm road where Everly wanted me to land," he said.

"I don't see anyone around. No planes. No cars."

"No people. That's good. No one to report having seen us."

"But if we crash—"

"We're not going to crash. I know what I'm doing. I thought you said you trusted me."

"I said that, yes. And I do. Now…just focus on landing."

Brett flipped switches and pushed buttons and Kinsley squeezed her eyes closed as the road came up to meet them. The plane bounced hard and lifted on the right side, then settled, still bobbing and jolting on the uneven ground. When the plane stopped, she opened her eyes.

I can finally breathe.

And took in a big, long breath. Brett squeezed her hand and she turned to look at him.

He smiled.

How could he smile at a time like this? Was

this some kind of game to him? "Oh, I get it. This was actually fun to you."

She ripped off the headset and hopped out. Looked like Brett had steered the plane to the side of the road as much as possible.

He tossed their packs on the ground and met her under the wing. "Let's get moving before someone comes to check this out."

"Fine then. Which way do we go to get to the car your sister had delivered for us?"

"This way," he said, and they gathered up their packs. After about twenty minutes of walking, he abruptly pointed. "It's just there under the trees. At least I hope it's the car she promised."

Kinsley was suddenly infused with hope they could actually survive. After the unexpected encounter in the cave had thrown their plans off course, she'd begun to doubt everything. Except Brett. She wouldn't doubt him when it came to protecting her and helping her.

Why'd you let me go?

She stared at the road ahead and shoved those thoughts away.

With his longer strides, Brett hiked in front of her but glanced over his shoulder, then turned around to walk backward, amusement dancing in his eyes. He *was* actually enjoying this. Or maybe, like her, he felt encouraged they had made it out. With Everly's help, they had a way to safety, and they would eventually be able to relax and catch their breath once they made it to the safe house.

The sound of a helicopter drew their eyes to the sky.

"Hurry," he said. "Let's get out of here."

Brett turned to face ahead. Together, packs in tow, they ran toward the car beneath the trees. She pushed her legs, the pack bouncing against her side, then scrambled to the passenger side door, but it was locked.

"The fob should be in the wheel rim," Brett said.

Kinsley started searching with him. "That helicopter sounds close. Do you think it's searching for us?"

"Let's hope not."

"Maybe this isn't the vehicle," Kinsley said.

"This is the right one."

"There!" Kinsley gasped. "On the ground beneath the car, right next to the wheel."

Brett reached under the car and grabbed the fob, immediately unlocking the car. Kinsley opened the door and tossed her pack in the back seat as did Brett. Then he hopped in, started the vehicle.

But he didn't speed away like she expected.

"What are you waiting for?"

He lowered the window. "For the helicopter to

head away. I don't want to draw their attention by driving out from the trees. It would blow the whole reason of switching the plane for this."

The helicopter sounded distant, but it could come back or be informing the police or someone else about the downed plane just a mile down the road. Brett steered them out of the trees and onto the road.

"Where are we going?"

"I need to get away from the area, so the helicopter won't spot us when it comes back. In the meantime, text Everly—"

A notification dinged. "Sounds like she might have texted you."

He tossed her the satellite phone. "What does it say?"

"It's coordinates for an off-grid cabin."

"Can you add them to the car's navigation system?"

"Sure thing."

After she'd entered the coordinates, the navigation system directed him to turn around back toward the plane. Brett kept going instead.

"You're not going to the cabin?"

"I'm going to take the long way around. The system will recalculate our route. We can't risk going anywhere near that plane. We have to blend in."

"This whole thing seems surreal. I can't believe I'm a fugitive, on the run for my life and I dragged you, of all people, into this with me. I've changed my appearance, been followed anyway, tracked through a cave and almost ambushed, spent a cold night in the wilderness, escaped in a plane, and now we're going to hide again in an off-grid cabin. I don't know how much more of this I can take."

"If anything, Kinsley, you've proved that you're a survivor. And you're going to make it."

"*We're* going to make it, Brett. I couldn't have done this without help." *Without you.*

"Once we get to the cabin, I know Everly will have included all that we need to learn the truth, and she is probably searching on her own. We'll find the evidence we need soon. We'll figure out who is behind this so you won't have to hide anymore. You won't have to fear for your life."

Fear for your life...

What would she have done if Brett wasn't in this with her?

As if sensing she needed reassurance, Brett reached across the console between them and squeezed her hand. "It's going to be okay."

Kinsley liked the feel of his strong grip and the reassurance that flooded her—a little too much.

Maybe she wasn't afraid of losing her life with him by her side, but she was definitely afraid of losing her heart.

* * *

While a frozen casserole baked in the oven, Brett came back inside from checking the perimeter one last time. He finally felt like he could relax. He never doubted Everly's ability to find a safe place for them to stay—and he also wasn't surprised that the house possessed all the amenities for comfort. Someone had thought through all the variables and contingencies to keep them off-grid but still hi-tech. Someone who didn't want to be uncomfortable while enjoying their nature getaway. The house also had a robust satellite link to the internet and Kinsley had already settled in, continuing to search through the Steven's Lab database.

For what, he didn't know. And she admitted, she didn't either.

She'd taken a spot at the dining table between the kitchen and living area, and he passed her on the way to the kitchen to check on the casserole. He could already smell it and it should be ready in a few minutes.

"Don't freak out if you happen to open the fridge. I put the wafers in the fridge. They're in their own protective container, but my cool storage baggie is all out of cool. The fridge will be just the right temperature for them since it's the same temperature as the caves. I hope that's okay." She smiled but didn't glance away from her computer.

"I'll try to ignore them when I open the refrigerator. You're such a nerd," he teased. "Usually, people are trying to avoid having a science project in their fridges."

"If I had something to throw, I'd throw it at you." She laughed, but it sounded strained. "Listen, Brett. I still need to get to the university lab to start processing through what I collected. In the end, this could provide us with answers. I admit, those answers will be a long time in coming, but it can't hurt to be working on this while we look at everything else too."

Yeah. About that... "I don't think it's safe for you to go to the lab just yet."

"What?" Now she stopped staring at the computer screen to look at him. "How am I supposed to—"

He held up his hand, hoping to silence her. "I know what you're going to say, but think it through. The men searching for you were *expecting* you to show up at the cave. Where else would they expect you to go?"

She stood from the chair and stretched. "You think they're going to be watching any possible lab where I could work as well now." Kinsley plopped back in the chair. "You're right. At least the specimens will keep in storage until I can get to them. It's just that... I don't want to lose what Max gained in his work. That's still important, even if what I collected today ends up having nothing to do with helping us discover who killed Max." She dropped her head and closed her eyes. "I hadn't considered that, really, until this moment. If I make it through this, maybe I can somehow continue his work. He's all I have left. This...is all I have left."

Oh, Kinsley. His heart ached for her.

She huffed an incredulous laugh. "The lab is gone and all I have left is the microscopic creatures I collected yesterday and the data. I know that in addition to the off-site servers, Max stored information in the cloud. I'm assuming he uses the same login. I should look into those files and see if I can find anything. . She lifted her nose and drew in a long inhale. "That smells wonderful. When will it be ready?"

"Soon." *Though not soon enough.* He moved into the kitchen to check on the timer and peeked in the oven. The cheese was just starting to bubble on the top.

Behind him, fingers tapped against the keyboard again. Brett moved to look over her shoulder as she sat at the table. Her hair smelled like vanilla wrapped in Kinsley's own personal scent—they'd cleaned up first thing after arriving at the safe house—and Brett couldn't help thinking about how much he wanted to wrap her in his arms.

But he couldn't do that to her. She was vulnerable now. They both were. And after it was over, he wouldn't hurt them both again. Instead, he would get the help he needed to put the nightmares aside. He was damaged goods until he did.

"Interesting." Her tone drew his attention back. "There are emails here instead of reports. External emails instead of data."

Kinsley gasped.

Brett stared at the screen. "What's the matter?"

"The screen locked up. I refreshed and now half the files are gone!"

"What did you do? What's happening?"

"Oh! No, no, no, no! Someone else knows about this and is deleting them. I need to download as much as I can onto this machine."

Kinsley rushed down to the bottom and tried to download the files, but the laptop continued to process—and satellite internet link wasn't as fast as if they were hardwired—so it was taking much too long. Brett had a very bad feeling about this. By the time she refreshed the page, the files were completely gone.

She growled and bolted from the chair. "Who could know his log-in and where to find his files? Who is behind this?"

"I put Everly on that earlier, when the first files went missing."

"Good. Smart. Thank you. See, it must have something to do with the new bacteria he's cultivating and his research on potential therapies."

"What therapies, Kinsley? Maybe that's key?"

She shook her head. "At this stage in the process, it isn't really possible to narrow it down to a specific therapy. I can't believe anyone would target the lab for that. They've stolen files, so they want the organisms, but they just didn't want Max to profit from his research. I have a feeling that whoever is behind this is not going to stop until I'm dead!" She bolted from the chair and moved to the spacious living room to pace.

Brett wanted to calm her, but he honestly had no idea how to reassure her. It seemed like she needed space to figure this out and he had nothing to offer. He was deeply concerned that she was right about how far someone would go to get her out of the way.

He moved to the kitchen, wishing the lasagna would be ready. He peeked in the fridge at her science project, then closed the door.

Cold.

Storage.

He turned as she approached him in the kitchen. Perfect timing. "You said Max stored certain files on the cloud. A lot of people also use cold storage—or rather, an external hard drive. If he was that diligent, he probably also has a hard drive kept in a location other than the lab for extra security. Where would he keep it? At home?"

She stared at him. "If he kept it at the lab, then it's gone. If he kept it at home, then someone would have gotten it already." She moved back to pacing. "I have to think."

Brett wouldn't disturb her. He went to check on the lasagna again. There were only five minutes left on the timer, and a glance in the oven told him it was ready now. With pot holders, he pulled it out of the oven. The mundane task helped him to calm his racing heart and chaotic thoughts.

God, how do I protect her? Who is behind this?

Kinsley entered the kitchen; her blue-green eyes snagged his and her expression was thoughtful.

"You know something." He set the casserole on the counter.

"Maybe. We went to grab a fast lunch a few weeks ago and Max made a quick stop at the gym. He said he had to do something. He went in with his workout duffel and left it there."

"You think he left a hard drive in a locker at the gym?"

"I don't know. It could be a rabbit trail we don't need to follow. But I'm not sure where else he might keep it if it even exists. So, it's something. It's a start. I'll keep thinking."

She glanced at the lasagna. "Is that ready? I'm hungry."

"It needs time to cool."

"Does it, now. You've become quite the cook."

Was she actually smiling at him? During their deep discussion? "It was a frozen premade casserole that I put in the oven. I read the instructions on the package. Uh—don't even say it."

"Okay. I won't say I'm surprised that you actually read the instructions."

"Some men do, you know."

"Duly noted. I'll just grab the dishes while we're waiting on it to cool." She opened a cabinet and reached inside, grabbing two stoneware plates.

"Thanks," he said. "About the hard drive— if it's at the gym, how can we figure out which locker is his? How would we even get into it?"

Kinsley set the plates on the table. She'd grabbed utensils too. "I don't know. This is all so maddening."

"Maybe. But I think you're onto something."

"I'm just desperate," she said. "Maybe the

only way for me to discover the truth is make myself bait. I need to turn myself in and see what happens."

What had gotten into her? "No way am I going to let you do that, Kinsley. It's too dangerous."

"We might not have a choice." She crossed her arms.

"We're not there yet. There must be another way." Now Brett paced. "What about Max's aunt you mentioned earlier? Where does she live?"

"In a suburb in Tacoma, the last I heard. I don't think he liked her much but she was his only family that I know of. I joined Max for Thanksgiving at her house a total of two times, I think. She was kind of cantankerous and critical. At least what I remember of her.""Sounds like Max didn't see her that often. That might be the perfect place to hide his hard drive if he felt that the data was important. He might have even known that trouble was coming his way." He was reaching for something that might not exist, but they had to try.

"What about the gym?"

"If Aunt Paula's is a bust, then we can try to break into his locker at the gym."

She nodded. "I guess we could see if he left something at her house. But what if they're watching there too?"

"That's a risk, but we need answers, and we'll have to take our chances."

"You sound like me when it came to going to the cave, Brett. What's happening?"

"I'm getting desperate, and like you said last night—desperate measures… "

"Yeah, about that. You know I didn't mean it that way."

Yeah, he knew that she didn't have to be desperate to cozy up to him to keep warm. But she truly had been desperate.

"What if Everly could go talk to her instead?"

She arched a brow. "I…don't think she's going to let a stranger inside. I think I need to be the one."

He nodded. That made sense. "We'll stake out her house and, if it looks safe, *then* we'll get inside and speak to her. It'll mean leaving the safe house and if we're not here then we could run into danger."

"But we have to do this. The other issue is that Paula might call the police on us, even though she knows me."

"When did she meet you last?"

"It's been years."

"She might not even recognize you then," he said. "Everly created an alias for us to use if needed."

"Let's say we wear disguises and use our

aliases so she won't recognize me. Or us, since we're all over the news. Then what do we say to her?" Kinsley asked.

"That we were friends of Max's and we're sorry for her loss."

She shrugged. "I think that could work."

"So we have a plan for tomorrow. Tonight, we rest up from our rough day of hiking and camping in the wilderness and our wild escape in an out-of-fuel plane."

He moved the lasagna over to the table and grabbed a knife and spatula, then put a healthy portion of lasagna on each plate. Grabbed glasses of water and set those on the table too.

Kinsley took a seat, and Brett bowed his head to say grace.

"This looks delicious," she said. "I'm starving."

"Lasagna hits the spot every time."

"Your sister really is the best."

"Yeah, she is. She's engaged to be married to an old boyfriend. They'd dated years ago and their paths crossed again when he hired her to help protect his daughter. So they got back together." Oh, man. That story sounded much too similar to his current situation with Kinsley. He didn't want to bring up their past together.

He stuck the too-hot lasagna in his mouth, to keep himself from saying more.

They continued eating in silence—both of them too hungry to have a conversation. He was glad for the distraction of food, except it didn't do anything to stop him from thinking about his past with Kinsley.

That moment he'd gone with his team to Bangladesh, rescued her family and transported them to safety. Something about the blue-green-eyed auburn-haired young woman with a splash of freckles across her nose had snagged him. They'd exchanged cell phone numbers and emails and their relationship had continued through remote communication until he had gotten leave, and the next thing he knew, he was visiting her at University of Washington in Seattle where she was attending school.

And then that kiss.

Their first kiss had been so sweet, and he'd thought…he'd thought… *This is the woman I want to marry.*

But he'd ruined it all.

Kinsley set her fork down on her plate, and it clanked a little too loudly. He stared at the fork, then lifted his gaze to hers.

"Maybe this isn't the best time," she said, "but there's not going to be a perfect time. And maybe we don't need to have this conversation, but I would really like to know, Brett. I would love to understand. That way I can put this to rest and move on."

She hadn't put their relationship to rest? Neither had he.

"It's the big elephant in the room that we dance around," she continued. "You broke things off with me three years ago without any explanation. I'd like to know why. I thought you cared about me."

A knot lodged in his throat. *And... I still do.*

FOURTEEN

Could she be any more ridiculous? Why bring this up now? It shouldn't matter anymore. Elbows on the table against her better manners, she pressed her face into her palms.

Her heart pounded, sending her pulse roaring in her ears. "Forget I asked that. I'm too exhausted to have a filter right now. My question was inappropriate and it doesn't matter."

She dropped her hands but stared at her plate. She didn't want to face him now that she'd blurted that out.

"It's on your mind," he said. "So it matters. I tell you what, you have a couple bites left. Promise me you'll finish your dinner because you need the sustenance and it's delicious—" he sent her that adorable grin "—and I promise that I'll explain after dinner."

She frowned and stared at her lasagna. How was she supposed to finish? "I'm not a child, Brett. Besides, I can't eat any more."

From across the table, he pressed his hand over hers again—his touch was gentle and soothing. It made her miss what they had before. *No...* Still, she didn't move it away.

"Okay. I'll tell you and then we can put this behind us." His grin was tenuous, nervous.

But Kinsley refused to return the smile. "I shouldn't have asked." *What are you doing, Kinsley?* Trying to ruin their ability to work together during this intolerable death trap?

Kinsley helped him clean up. She washed the plates and utensils and put them away. The house had a dishwasher but there weren't enough dishes to bother using it. Brett had put foil over the lasagna and stuck it in the fridge with her "science project."

Dinner over and dishes done, the moment of truth was upon them. Kinsley felt nothing but dread at the thought of their planned conversation.

"Look, Brett. I changed my mind. I don't want to know. It's better if we just move on. We don't need to talk about it." *And I don't want to be hurt all over again.*

"You brought it up. You haven't moved on after three years. Not really." A slight frown creased his brows. "And honestly, neither have I. I want to explain, Kinsley. I've wanted to tell you everything for a while. Give me the chance."

She risked a look at his eyes and saw the same heartache she felt. The same regret. "Okay. I guess I do need to know. We're here now. For some inexplicable reason, we've been thrown back together. Maybe it's because we both needed the chance to forgive and forget and finally move on." Her voice cracked on those last words. And really, what had she done that he should forgive her? He'd been the one to stun her with the breakup.

Heading to the sofa, she plopped down. She tugged the folded blanket from the back and pulled it over her while Brett stoked the fire. A strange romantic ambience filled the space, and her heart rate kicked up.

I don't want to know what happened before. But I need to know.

Brett took his time and she suspected that he was measuring his words and deciding how much of the story he would share. Would he tell her the truth? Or make something up to ease her pain and his guilt? Warrant Officer Brett Honor—the man she'd fallen in love with.

The man who'd broken her heart.

Now here she was depending on him, trusting him with her life.

No matter what he said to her, she wouldn't trust him with her heart.

Don't trust him. Don't fall for him again.

No matter what.

Brett sat in the cushy chair across from her. The sun had set, and the firelight cast shadows on his face.

"I was piloting the helicopter that crashed and killed my gunner—who'd become like a brother to me. He was just a kid—to me, anyway—and I… I tried to protect him. The crash left me with ashattered femur, but I still had my life."

Kinsley gasped. "Brett, you never told me! Why didn't you tell me? You told me that you were going on a mission and wouldn't be able to talk for a while. The next time I heard from you…"

He shook his head. "I was in the worst kind of place mentally and emotionally. I was mad at God, and I just couldn't accept what happened, believing that if I'd done something differently, Kevin would still be alive."

Kinsley struggle to breathe. Oh, Brett. "I'm so so sorry." *I didn't know…* Her heart ached for him. She had no more words to offer, and they sat in silence for a few more moments. Then she realized… She could have been there for him. Prayed for him. Supported him. *I would have come to you in the hospital.* Instead, at the worst time of his life, he'd kept the truth from her. Pushed her away.

She thought she couldn't be hurt more, but

she had been wrong. This was painful news to add onto the breakup.

Elbows on his thighs, he leaned forward and hung his head. A few moments later, he lifted his face. Held her gaze. "I thought I didn't have anything to offer you. I didn't want to put you through so much suffering with me. You'd lost your parents, Kinsley."

His frown deepened as he continued to hold her gaze. She could sense his sincerity—but at the same time, it unsettled her that he seemed to think she needed to be protected from grief. She knew how to handle it—all too well. Her sister had died from a rare virus when they were just kids, and that had driven her parents to work with Doctors Without Borders. Driven Kinsley to become a biologist and try to make the world a safer place, in her own way. Brett hadn't known Olivia personally, but he had known what had happened to her. While she'd never been in a combat situation, she still felt she would have understood what he'd been feeling, and surely that understanding could have helped him heal. Why hadn't he given her the opportunity?

"But Mom and Dad died two years earlier. You went through that with m. At least you were there for me emotionally, even though you were overseas and couldn't come back for the funeral. I didn't keep it from you, Brett. So I don't understand. I could have been there for *you*. I could have helped you through it. We could have worked through it together and who knows, we might have stayed together. I mean, neither of us can know what would have happened between us, but I can't see this as a reason to call things off. Don't you realize how much you hurt me?"

"I hurt myself too, but I was in such a bad place that I couldn't think straight, and I made a colossal mistake. After ending things with you, I shattered my own heart, and I was doubly broken. All I could see in my head was the last moments of the crash. They played over and over in my mind. All I could hear was Kevin's dying screams. So, in the end, you deserved better than me. Looking back, of course, I regret my decision but not for the reasons you think. I regret that it was the only choice I could make. I'm damaged goods, Kinsley. I was a mess then, and I'm a mess now."

She ached for the gut-wrenching grief he obviously still felt inside. The flashbacks that must feel debilitating at times.

How do I help him?

He held her gaze. And with that look, He was he trying to tell her without words that this growing feeling between them—what she'd been trying to push aside, what he was probably feeling too—could not be explored—because he still had too many problems.

Kinsley closed her eyes and tried to wrap her mind around all he'd gone through. Tried to understand from his point of view, but she could never understand. She blew out a long breath. "I can't blame you for what you did, Brett, but neither do I understand it. Still, a person doesn't know what they'll do, how they'll react until they're in a certain situation, so I won't hold it against you." But if he'd only made a different choice, they could have been together. Maybe.

Then again, maybe they would have broken up by now for any number of reasons. "What else can you tell me?"

"After I recovered, I was honorably discharged, and I decided to join the Coast Guard. It would keep me busy, and I wanted to be stateside. Eventually, Ayden talked me into joining HPS. Ayden had been through some job-related trauma with the Diplomatic Security Service, and he understood that I might have been still suffering from PTSD."

Brett sat back and closed his eyes.

Kinsley gave him the time to say more.

And he did. "A few months ago I was in another helicopter crash. In the immediate aftermath, I thought I was doing okay, but eventually,

it started eating at me. I started having flashbacks again. Ayden gave me the choice to see
a therapist or to step back and take some time
away. I was supposed to go to Fiji, but I wanted
to stick closer. It seems crazy that I was here
when you called so I could help you. Honestly,
I thought you'd have forgotten me completely,
would maybe even be married by now."

Seriously? She never could have forgotten
him. But her feelings for him were even more
complicated now. She couldn't blame him for
breaking up with her when he was so messed
up, but now that she understood his reasons, she
still couldn't get involved with him again because he still needed help. Flashbacks and grief,
blaming himself for what happened before, he'd
just keep sabotaging any relationship he was in.
She still couldn't trust him completely to not
hurt her again.

"I threw all my energy into finding drugs
with Max so I could save lives." *And not have
to think about how hurt I was.* Kinsley got off
the sofa. "Thanks for telling me the truth, Brett.
I'm going to turn in now. I'll see you in the
morning. Let's hope tomorrow is the day we
end this."

So she could end this brief moment in her life
she had to spend with Brett. He was like a virus
trying to get under her skin and into her heart.

* * *

The next morning, after a fitful night, Brett and Kinsley set out from the safe house to learn more. Brett steered up I-5 toward the Tacoma suburb where Max's aunt lived. They had put aside the possibility that Max had stored the hard drive in his gym locker, for now.

To add to her disguise of shorter brown hair, Kinsley wore a beanie along with her glasses, changing up her disguise only slightly from the days before. And Brett now wore square glasses and sunglasses over those—*just call me six-eyes*—and a Western shirt, Wranglers with a rodeo belt buckle, along with a Stetson— compliments of Everly. He'd laughed when he opened the closet and found the new disguise. His sister had a gift, that was for sure.

She also had the gift of sensing when something was a bad idea, and she hadn't held back when she'd warned him this was a risky maneuver. He agreed 100 percent, but they were running out of time to find the truth. Kinsley couldn't hide out forever, and in fact, neither could Brett. He would need to return to work next week.

Actual, *official* work at Honor Protection Specialists.

He almost laughed at that. Though he wasn't officially working, neither had he taken time off, after all, because he was helping Kinsley. But helping her had been the medicine he needed to pull out of his funk. While he'd wanted to tell her everything for the longest time, he felt a little awkward with her today. She glanced at him now and then, and he wondered what she was thinking. Was she scared of him because of his struggle?

He hoped she knew that he would protect her and keep her safe, and give his life for her, if needed. He almost wished he hadn't been so completely open. But at least that was done and over with.

Regardless, Kinsley seemed sadder and more distant to him today after he'd told her the truth.

I wouldn't have thought that.

In fact, he kind of expected her to be more understanding. Still, her cold shoulder was a good thing because Brett wasn't a stable enough guy for her to get involved with. She shouldn't risk it.

And neither should he.

Still, there was another element at play here. Since coming to her aid, he hadn't had a single nightmare about what happened before. He could beat himself up repeatedly for letting her go, but he couldn't change the past. Since he was doing much better while with her, he had to admit that deep inside, part of him had hoped this was a second chance with her.

Why bring us back together, Lord, if we're not supposed to be together?

Because this was pure torture.

But God certainly knew better than Brett. Maybe he was simply the man needed to help Kinsley during this desperate time in her life. She was still alive and Brett would do everything in his power to keep her that way.

The navigation system directed them to take a few turns, and Brett purposefully avoided turning down the road where the house was located.

"What are you doing? She lives down that way."

"I want to stake out the place. Remember?"

"Are you going to walk through that neighborhood dressed like a cowboy? You'll stand out and draw attention."

Maybe she was right and Everly had chosen his disguise to tease him without thinking through every nuance. He would have to tease *her* about it in turn. "I don't want to give away our vehicle and risk someone following us again. We need to be able to return to the safe house…safely."

"Well, remove the hat, and you're still unrecognizable. Park on the other side of the neighborhood and we can walk through together like a couple making our way to the park over there."

"That's a great idea." He couldn't help but smile at that. "You're getting the hang of this."

And her smile back to him warmed him through and through. Maybe her cold shoulder was growing warm. Uh. Oh. That was a dangerous thought. He was better off focusing on what they were there to accomplish. "Let's do this."

He steered the vehicle around to the neighborhood on the far side and found a convenience store where he parked in the farthest spot. He hopped out and Kinsley joined him.

"Ready?" he asked, holding out his hand.

She looked at his offered hand as if reconsidering the plan, then finally placed hers in his. Her grip was strong, but her hand was small. Her skin was soft and the touch stirred him in ways he'd prefer to ignore.

"It's going to be okay, Kinsley. We're going to find the truth and get justice for Max and keep you safe while we do it."

Brett searched the area as they walked, then tugged her closer. "We're supposed to be a couple, right? We'll draw less attention if we're wrapped up in each other."

"You're making that up."

"No, really. We'll be less noticeable if we're standing close, than if we're two people walking along."

"I still don't believe you, but it's okay." They crossed the street to Paula's neighborhood and walked along the sidewalk, passing by beautiful thick juniper bushes and cedars. The clouds had moved in for a typical rainy day, and it started to drizzle.

"So after this is over, do you really think you'll rebuild Max's lab and continue on the path he started?"

"I haven't thought that far ahead, honestly. When I mentioned it last night, that was the first time for it to cross my mind. It's hard to wrap my mind around. It could be that NewBio will simply absorb the lab's work. I don't know what contractual obligations are in place if something were to ever happen to the lab—say an explosion took it out."

"You could start your own lab."

"Maybe, but honestly, I can't think about that yet. We're almost up to her house. Have you seen anyone suspicious yet?"

"No. But I thought natural conversation would help with the disguise. Thanks for humoring me."

"Oh, and here I thought you were really interested."

"I was. I am." He pulled her closer.

But she shifted away. "Her house is up on the left. Let's do this now. No sense in putting it off."

Brett would prefer to stake the place out for

a day or two before even approaching, but they didn't have the time. *It's now or never.*

They strode up the sidewalk to the house, up the steps to the porch and Kinsley knocked on the door.

It swung open to reveal Lee Jackson. He pointed a handgun at Brett.

FIFTEEN

Kinsley's heart jumped to her throat. This couldn't be happening.

Lee waved the gun, urging them forward. She couldn't believe they'd escaped him—in a plane—just to run into him here. Then again, she shouldn't be surprised.

"Both of you, step inside," Lee growled. "Nice and slow. Reach for that gun and you're dead."

For a split second, Brett stiffened, and Kinsley suspected he was weighing his options. Would Brett lunge at him? Disarm him? Something?

"You too, Kinsley," Lee said. His thick bushy brows furrowed over angry eyes.

Brett kept her pushed behind him as they entered, and Lee backed away, keeping enough distance between them that Brett couldn't disarm him or reach him before he could shoot.

They stood in the middle of the dimly lit living room. Kinsley noticed that Paula was nowhere to be seen and fear for the woman almost paralyzed her.

Lee once again waved the gun, using it to enforce his will. "Now slowly take your gun out of the holster, along with any knives or other weapons, and set them on the floor."

"What do you want with us?" Brett asked.

Jackson lifted his aim to Kinsey's head. "Do as I say or she dies now."

She dies now...*as opposed to later?* Brett removed his handgun from the holster hidden under his jacket, and slowly crouched to set it on the floor. Kinsley expected him to try something and was almost disappointed when he stood without taking action.

"Now kick it over."

Brett continued to comply and kicked the gun over. "Again, what do you want with us?"

Ignoring Brett, Lee stared at Kinsley. "You've already caused me too much trouble."

"Where's Paula?" she asked. "What did you do to her?"

"That old lady? Why do you care?"

"Listen, you." Brett growled as he stepped forward, his hands fisted. "You're not going to get away with this."

"That's a cliché. People get away with stuff all the time."

This guy wasn't going to let them live. Why

didn't he just kill them now? But she had a feeling she knew—he intended to make it look like an accident, like she'd heard the other men mention at the wilderness campsite . Like she heard at the lab—it had been made to look like an accident, only Kinsley hadn't died and too many questions were being asked. Here, there were way too many options for Lee to kill them in a manner that wouldn't look suspicious. Though he had followed them before, now he was here to finish business.

Would he shoot them first?

Heart pounding, Kinsley had to persuade him to let them go. "I don't know anything, okay? Just leave us alone."

"Get down on the floor, on your stomachs." Execution style.

Oh, Lord, please help us. Her whole body shook. They were going to die. There wasn't a way to escape this. She glanced at Brett, hoping to get reassurance from him, but he didn't look her way. The only sign he was distressed was the vein bulging at his temple.

We're going to die, really going to die.

Tears surged from her eyes. Why had she insisted they go to the house now? Why had Brett listened to her?

God, please help us. She would keep praying until He answered her prayer—one way or another.

Kinsley started to get on the floor so this guy could execute them, but hesitated. "Can I at least know what this is all about before you kill me?"

Lee opened his mouth to reply

Brett kicked the gun out of Jackson's hand, and it flew across the room and hit the wall. Brett and Lee both dove for Brett's gun on the floor, and they grabbed it simultaneously.

The battle was on. Whoever got control of that gun was going to shoot it. Going to win.

I can't let Jackson kill us.

Brett had given them a chance to turn this around. Maybe her question had been just the distraction he'd needed.

Do something! She was moving way too slowly. Wasn't practiced at quick tactical responses. But right now, she would take action. She rushed to the other side of the room to find Jackson's gun.

There. Between the couch and the wall on the floor.

She got down on the floor and reached under the sofa. Gripping it, she slid it out. Then chambered a round. Adrenaline spiked through her as she turned to see the two men still grappling for the other gun.

Kinsley knew how to use a gun, but she wasn't a skilled marksman, and she knew she should only aim a loaded weapon if she intended to shoot someone.

A figure appeared from the hallway.

Paula! And the older woman held up a big cast-iron pan. A Chihuahua dashed around the corner yapping and growling.

Lee secured the gun from Brett and jumped up, stepping back away from him, aiming the gun. Kinsley feared he would shoot Brett, but before he had the chance, Paula slammed the pan down on their attacker's head.

Dropping the gun, he stumbled back, but somehow kept his bearings. Paula stepped out of the way, scowling at him. She lifted the pan as if she was going to whack him again. Kinsley lowered her handgun because she didn't want to accidentally shoot the wrong person. Then Lee fled through the kitchen.

"Hey!" Brett scrambled to his feet, grabbed his handgun that Lee had dropped, then followed the man through the kitchen, the Chihuahua chasing him.

The door banged twice.

"Chester, come back here!" Paula disappeared into the kitchen too.

Kinsley wanted to shout those same words at Brett—*Come back here!*—but he'd run after the man who'd followed them, hoping to get answers. Chester hurried back into the living room like a good dog, but Brett didn't follow. Paula picked Chester up with one hand and still held on to her weapon—the big cast-iron pan—in the other. Strong woman.

Kinsley lowered the gun she held. "Paula. I'm Kinsley Langell. Do you remember me? I worked with Max."

Paula was in her late seventies and had long silver hair, and her lips seemed to be perpetually pursed. She squinted her eyes and looked more closely at Kinsley. "You changed your look. I don't have to guess why. Sure, I know who you are, and I know who your friend is too. I watch the news. But I don't know who the other guy is. He claimed he was with the police so I let him in. That was my mistake. Now, what are you doing here?"

"We need your help."

"I can't get involved. I can't help a fugitive. The police are looking for you." Paula set Chester down. "Now, where did he hide my cell? I need to call the police."

"Please," Kinsley said. "That's not a good idea."

"Oh, really, why is that?"

"It's not what you think."

"What is it you believe I think?"

"If you watch the news, they're spinning it that I might be responsible for Max's death."

"You're running and hiding from the police, so you can understand why people might believe that, but the man I hit in the head, he was here waiting on you. I think I know why you're running from the police. That one is a dirty one, though I'm not sure he's a police officer after all. What police officer would tie an old lady and her dog up and leave them in the closet? We've been in there since last night."

"He was *waiting* on us to come here next? Wow." Kinsley eased onto the sofa. Paula was Max's only living relative, and Lee expected them to question her. He obviously understood that Kinsley was trying to find evidence and answers.

"Even if he's not police, he's still connected somehow," Brett said as he entered the living room from the kitchen, gasping for breath. He glanced at Kinsley. "He got away. With all the dogs barking, I was drawing too much attention. We need to get out of here."

"Not without answers. Lee tied her up and locked her in the closet with Chester."

Brett's eyes widened. "I'm glad to see that you're okay now. You *are* okay, aren't you?"

"We're fine. Just a little sore, a little shook up and not a little mad."

Kinsley almost smiled at that. "I'm glad you

were mad because you know how to hit a man with a pan."

That made Paula laugh. "I wanted to hit him again. I'd still be in that closet if it wasn't for Chester. He chewed himself free, and then helped me."

"He's a smart dog."

"The best." Paula smiled as if they were all partners-in-fighting-criminals together. Then her smile shifted to a deep frown. "I can't believe Max is gone."

Paula slowly sat down.

Kinsley sat next to her. "I know. I can't either... I need you to understand that I didn't kill Max. Whoever killed him thought I was in the lab and wanted to kill me too. I overheard their conversation and I know someone in the PD is involved. I just need to find evidence."

"And you came here thinking I might *know* something?"

Kinsley shrugged. "Not know something, really, but I hoped you might have something that belongs to Max. Could he have hidden something here? Kept something here?"

Paula's smile shifted back to pursed lips. "I don't think so. He didn't come by that often, so why would he leave anything here?"

Kinsley's shoulders sagged. "When was the last time he was here?"

"A month ago. Wait. He also stopped by two weeks ago. That's a record."

"I thought you said he didn't come that often."

"His visits weren't regular. Before that, I hadn't seen him in six months."

Brett pulled out his cell. "We don't have time for this, Kinsley. Jackson could come back and with his friends this time. I need to call Everly in case we need another way out."

Instead of the car? Kinsley could tell that he was getting close to bringing in Honor Protection Specialists with or without her approval. And she was getting closer to the point where she might have no choice but to bring others in, even if she still believed that the fewer people who knew, the safer they would all be. As a scientist she recognized that isolating a virus was the best way to keep it from spreading, and right now, Kinsley was that virus.

She needed to keep this as contained as possible, and regretted coming to see Paula. But she was here and had to get the most out of this risk they'd taken.

"You said that Max was here two weeks ago. Do you mind if I just look around to see if he left anything?"

"What are you looking for? Maybe I can help."

"It would be small. We think he might have

left a hard drive, um…the size of an index card only thicker, or maybe a small USB thumb drive. The drive could hold important information that could point to who is behind his death."

"Let's get busy. If it's here, we'll find it."

Paula followed Kinsley around the house. Having her look over her shoulder made her nervous. "Is this what you did when Max was here? Follow him around?"

"Nah. He didn't walk around searching. He had a few books he liked, though. Over on the shelf. Would pull them out and flip through them while we talked. Sometimes sit and read for a while."

Kinsley's breath caught. She moved over to the bookshelf in the living room to have a closer look. Brett remained on his cell phone, sounding like he was in a hushed but heated argument.

"What books did he prefer?" Kinsley asked.

Paula let her finger roam over all the old thriller paperbacks, a few Tom Clancy novels— *Patriot Games, Clear and Present Danger*— and more. Others by Clive Cussler. Some old hardback classic mysteries by Rudyard Kipling and Sir Arthur Conan Doyle. All the books on the shelves were in the thriller or mystery genre—all except for one. A hardback novel, *Clan of the Cave Bears*. A person could buy a book specifically created to hide something, but none of these books were that. And then again, some people are all about do-it-yourself projects.

Kinsley opened *Clan of the Cave Bears* and flipped through.

Aha!

The back pages had been cut to offer a slot for a hard drive. Kinsley lifted it out and she caught Brett staring at her from across the room.

They'd found it.

Brett peeled out of the parking lot, then drove them to the freeway as quickly as possible.

Paula had been kind enough to herd them into the back seat of her vehicle in the garage. She'd opened the garage door with the automatic opener and driven them around the neighborhood and then parked next to their vehicle.

She was a strong woman and seemed to enjoy her role in this, acting as if it was a game and a mystery to be solved. But she agreed that she and Chester would go stay with a friend in Bellingham, a very northern part of Washington. Considering that Lee Jackson had a connection with a dirty cop, Paula was afraid to report his assault to the police. They had to find someone they could trust when the time was right—when they had enough evidence to prevent Paula and the two of them from both being locked up themselves and/or put in a dangerous and vulnerable position.

With each contact they made, they were putting more lives in danger.

He'd tried to convey that to Everly, but she was growing impatient with the secrecy. She'd said that she couldn't keep the fact she was working with them under wraps for much longer. She'd given them twenty-four hours to find hard evidence before letting their brothers know what was going on. In the meantime, she was searching for those behind the explosion and Max's death. Lincoln Mann, the detective that Honor Protection Specialists often worked with was already snooping around and asking questions. Everly had at least learned from Lincoln that the investigator on the case knew something else was going on and didn't like Kinsley for the murder.

That was a positive step in the right direction...unless it was a ruse to bring Kinsley in, making her believe she would be safe.

"Slow down, Brett." Kinsley's voice drew his attention back to her.

"You're driving too fast and will get us pulled over and then what?"

His thoughts had been twisting him up inside and his foot had responded by putting on the pressure. He eased off. Tried to relax. "You're right. Sorry."

"Back at Paula's, when I was looking for the hard drive, you were on your phone. You sounded like you and Everly were arguing."

"We were."

"I don't have to guess what that was about. She wants you to bring HPS in officially and also work with the police, yada yada yada."

He ground his teeth. "We have to find something soon, Kinsley. We're in over our heads."

To his surprise, she reached across the distance and put her hand on his arm. Her touch sent a warm current up his shoulder and across his chest, down to his heart.

"We'll find something," he said. "There must be an answer here. Max went to a lot of trouble to hide this. . But what if this isn't the only one."

"What do you mean?" she asked.

"He stopped in on Paula twice in one month. What if he was exchanging it?"

"You mean, you think he was switching the drive out for another one holding the latest data?"

"Yes, that could be the case. That means there are two. At least we have this one and we can look at it and find evidence. I hope."

"So where is the other one?" she asked.

"Could have been in the lab where he transferred the information or at his house or in the wrong hands. But we can't go to his house because—It could be under police surveillance," he said. "Or the men after you are watching it, anticipating you—we—might go there next. Just like Lee Jackson was waiting for us at Paula's."

"That's too bad." She pulled off her beanie and fluffed her hair.

"Chances are the guys after us didn't even know about this hard drive, if they have their hands on the other one. So it doesn't change anything for us." He changed lanes until he was in the far right lane and ready for their next exit.

"True. But if we don't have the only one, we can't be sure we have what we need. They might have the one with the evidence, when the other one has nothing. We can't know anything."

"Well, let's see what's on this drive." *I really want to wrap this investigation up and take down killers and let Kinsley get back to a life without danger.*

Another half hour driving along a two-lane road toward Mt. Rainier, and finally Brett turned into their safe house. No one had followed them, and Everly had used her technological skills to make sure no one could track this vehicle remotely.

After clearing the house, he made sure all the alarms were set and everything was in place.

But he still didn't feel comfortable. They'd risked a lot by showing their faces today and then coming back here. Someone could have been watching and he'd missed it. All the training in the world wasn't foolproof.

Kinsley grabbed them sodas and opened the laptop. "Let's see what's on this thing."

She connected it to her computer. "Oh, no. It's encrypted. Of course, it's encrypted. All this trouble and for what?"

"I know what we can do. I'm texting Everly now. She can get remote access to your laptop and break the encryption."

"If she can do *that*, then she *is* good."

"After everything you've seen, you doubted her? She's the best." He didn't know what HPS would do without Everly. "Okay, she wants me to put her on speakerphone and then she can instruct you how to let her get remote access to the laptop."

Brett took the back seat and watched as Kinsley worked with Everly. He'd never officially introduced them before. Hadn't introduced Kinsley to any of his family. At the time, they'd been spread out over the world. Ayden was in DSS, and Everly was working in the Tacoma PD. Caine was off in a jungle somewhere. Mom and Dad had died.

Kinsley seemed nervous, but Everly had a

way of making people relax. The next thing he knew, Kinsley and Everly were sharing jokes about Brett. All he could do was sit there and smile.

Except, this wasn't really a time to smile.

"Okay, Everly. I'm in." Kinsley focused on the computer screen.

"Good," Everly said. "I'll leave you two at it unless you want me to hang around."

"How about we call you when we find anything suspicious, or if we need more help?" Brett asked.

"I'll be around. Brett, can we talk privately? Sorry. Family business, Kinsley."

"Oh, no problem. I'll be working."

Brett snatched up the cell and turned it off speakerphone, putting it to his ear as he moved into the living room, dreading what he knew was coming.

"Lincoln's been asking a lot of questions. Obviously, you're in trouble and the local agencies have eyes on HPS. Meaning my help in the future is going to be limited. I've been able to put Lincoln off because he trusts me, but Ayden and Caine are demanding answers. Not that they don't trust me, but they're my brothers. They're *your* bothers and they're worried. And Lincoln answers to his superiors. We need to wrap this up as soon as possible."

"I hear you, sis. I would love to wrap this up soon too. Maybe have Lincoln try to figure out who could be the dirty police officer connected in all this. He would have to be subtle."

"I can't really ask him to do that unless I can give him all the information. He wouldn't even try unless he knew everything."

"And that can't happen yet. We'll be in touch." He ended the call, feeling the weight of the world on his shoulders.

God, we need answers.

"I'd love to meet her in person, Brett, after this is over." Kinsley focused on the laptop, skimming through files that she had opened from the hard drive.

Looking for what, he had no idea. He was no microbiologist. But maybe she could figure out what someone had killed Max over.

As for meeting Everly… "You'll love her."

What was he doing, making plans with Kinsley?

SIXTEEN

Hours later, Kinsley's eyes finally started glazing over as she stared at the computer screen. Weird how she could look into a microscope all day long, look at slides of strange tiny organisms and never grow tired of it, and yet, she would love to shut this laptop down.

Brett joined her at the table and set a bowl of barley soup in front of her.

"I think it's time to eat," he said. "Relax. You've been at this a long time. We've both been working too hard."

"With good reason." Blowing out a breath, she shoved the laptop to the far end of the table and pulled the bowl closer. Then sent a smile to Bret. He'd been more than patient with her. Hadn't asked a single question.

She stirred the soup.

"Found anything?" He lifted a spoon to his mouth.

Ah. There was the question.

"I mean…it's what I would expect to find, so nothing is jumping out at me. I don't get it, Brett. Why did he go to the trouble to hide a hard drive? Why did someone kill him? There has to be a connection. Maybe we've been going at this all wrong and his death, his murder, has nothing at all to do with microorganisms or his lab."

Kinsley ate a couple more bites. The soup was kind of bland but Brett didn't seem to mind, or if he did, he said nothing about it.

"I know people who go to extra lengths and keep hard drives at other places where they have nothing so dangerous to hide. Nothing worth killing for," he said. "People have all sorts of reasons that make sense to them, even if they're not clear to the rest of us. Maybe he left it with his aunt to give him an 'excuse' to see her. Visit her—twice in one month. Who knows? You made it sound like she wasn't an overly warm person, and at first, I would have agreed. But at the end there, she was all smiles and very helpful. I like her."'"

Kinsley laughed at that. "You know, I do too—even though I have to admit that I didn't before. I guess a person just has to give someone a chance, even if they think they don't like them at first."

"Or maybe being tied up and left in a closet

changes a person. Or being thrown into an action-packed murder mystery."

"We'll have to make an effort to go visit her after this is over and see how she is doing." *We?* "Anyway, back to the hard drive. Given the context, it seems the hard drive would have the answers we need."

"Why don't you let me look at it for a while, as soon as I finish eating?"

"I would love to hand it over, but you don't know what you're looking at," she said.

He lifted his spoon like he might a finger. "Exactly. Maybe something will stand out to me, that you simply skipped over."

Fair point. "It can't hurt, that's for sure. But I have another idea…" She let the words trail in a way that made Brett uneasily certain that he wasn't going to like her idea.

"More soup?" he asked.

"I can get it." She stood from the table and moved to the counter where he'd warmed three cans of soup in a pan. She ladled more into her bowl and waited for Brett to ask her for more information.

But he didn't ask. "Do you want to know my idea or not?" she asked.

She sat at the table again and dove into the soup. She hadn't realized how hungry she was.

"Sure. One thing I've learned, Kinsley, is that

if I wait patiently, you'll tell me in your own good time."

"Time is something we're running out of. On my idea... I've been thinking about this. We know that someone had access to Max's files. The only people outside of the Stevens Labs—which included exactly two people, me and Max—with that access are probably working at NewBio. I want to find a way into NewBio."

Brett stopped lifting his spoon midway to his mouth and stared. His eyes narrowed. "What are you saying?"

"We need to get inside. I need to physically go there so I can search for a reason someone at NewBio might have wanted to stop Max and his work. It's the only way, Brett."

He dropped his spoon back in the bowl. "The only way in like that is to take this to the police and get an investigator to look into things."

She slowly shook her head. "That's not the only way in. Max died. I almost died. I don't care what it takes, I want to find the answers. Even if someone in the PD wasn't dirty, I still wouldn't trust them to find the answers. This is a Big Pharma company, and they won't let anyone in who they don't want in. So we go in on our own." She couldn't believe her own ears. Had she really said that? She never imagined she could be this brazen, but the last few days had obviously changed her.

"Are you saying you want to break into the place?"

"Yes."

Brett pressed his lips into a thin line. "I think we've gone as far as we can go with this. Kinsley, it's time to officially bring in HPS."

"To protect me? Or to investigate? Either way, Brett, no one can get the answers that I can get."

The look he gave her made her think that he didn't agree with her. And maybe she wasn't making a lot of sense, but she wouldn't let this go.

"Breaking in would be illegal, Kinsley. That place is locked down like a fortress and it would take a lot of coordination and high-tech gadgets to get inside. We get caught, you'll definitely end up in a jail cell, and then what?"

"We?"

"Yes. Of course, we. What do you think, that I would let you do this alone?"

"So you're going to help me?"

"I'm here to help, but I don't think we are to the point where we need physical access to NewBio. First things first."

"What is there left to do?"

"The dishes." He grinned. "Then *I'm* going

to look at those files. And think. I need time to think."

"I'll do the dishes. You made dinner—it's only right that I clean up."

"Like there was anything to it. Heating up a few cans of soup is no effort at all."

"Cleaning the dishes—a couple of bowls and a pan—will require no effort either. I'm on it." Kinsley pointed at the laptop. "Get to it."

She grabbed their bowls along with the spoons and took them to the sink. Then washed them with warm soapy water. She grabbed the pan and ladle from the stove. It was empty because they had scraped it clean, getting the last of the soup. As she'd said, there wasn't much to clean up. After putting the bowls, utensils and pan away, she wiped down the kitchen counter and thought back to the time when she had dreamed of doing this kind of simple domestic activity as Brett's wife. What a silly girl she'd been. Those dreams seemed lofty, and yet this was a normal dream. Couples were getting married every day and settling into a life of bliss.

But that life wasn't for her, at least with Brett. With his confession that he still struggled with the same issues that caused him to break up before, he was basically confessing that he couldn't be trusted not to break her heart again. The problem was, Brett had been...the one. And even after three years, she hadn't found anyone else to take his place. She hadn't wanted to court love or take the risk again.

Until now.

Rubbing his tired eyes, Brett stared at the many files on the hard drive, skimming through them first. Later, he would go through each one with the fine-tooth comb if required. Maybe Everly should be the one to look at them. But he wouldn't push Kinsley on that point until he'd looked himself. Plus, Everly remained in the awkward position that he'd put her in. And Kinsley was starting to put Brett in an awkward position too. He was already in a precarious place, but her latest suggestion was going too far.

He swiped a hand down his face.

Break into NewBio? Really?

Illegal, illegal, illegal.

There had to be another answer. Another way. And he would find it before he let her risk everything on that crazy move. But he totally understood her desperation to get justice for Max, especially since her own life depended on it as well. Before he'd started on the computer, he texted Everly to find out if she'd learned anything about Lee Jackson, but he'd gotten no response yet. Either she was being monitored and couldn't respond or she didn't have the answers yet. Usually, it didn't take her long to get those.

Who are you, Lee Jackson? Was that really his name? Brett would do a bit of searching on his own when he was finished with these files.

Whatever they learned, there was no doubt the answers would not be found by going through the normal routes. With her expertise, Kinsley could very well be right that she was the one to find those answers.

Come on. What were you hiding, Max?

After skimming the too many files and data reports written in science so he couldn't understand, he stopped at a file labeled "emails." Huh. Kinsley had found a similar file on the cloud but its contents had been deleted before she could look at it. This could be something he could understand as he read, and maybe it would even contain what they had been looking for. Had Kinsley already seen these and looked at them? Or had she been so focused on the reports, searching for a novel drug reason for Max's death, that she missed them?

Kinsley was sitting on the sofa in the living room, resting while Brett opened and skimmed the emails. Max must have saved them here for a reason.

"I think I found something," he said, sometime later.

"What? How's that possible. You can't know what those reports mean." Kinsley bolted from the sofa and moved to stand over his shoulder. She peered at the screen.

"I'm not looking at the reports. I opened this file of emails." He opened one of the emails. "This one is from Carla Tempo."

Kinsley leaned in closer. "Wait a minute. Carla works at NewBio."

"Pull up a chair," he said. "We'll read them together."

I have a feeling about this.

His pulse quickened. They were onto something.

"Should we start with the first one?" she asked. "Or the last one?"

"I'll admit, it's this last one that has my attention."

The email simply read, "I'm scared."

Pressure built in his chest as he and Kinsley opened each one and read. Carla had communicated with Max about unethical behaviors at the company centering around fudged data. The list went on.

Kinsley slumped back against the chair. "It seems that Max's death had nothing to do with any of his discoveries or drugs with potential."

"And everything to do with what he learned is going on at NewBio," Brett said. "My big question is who is this woman and where is she now?"

"I say we use this email address and contact her to set up a meeting."

"No. Too risky. They killed Max and for all we know, she is on the lam. Let me get Everly involved to find her contact information and make sure it's safe to reach out." He waited for Kinsley's agreement, though really, this was the only safe move.

"Okay. Let Everly make sure she's safe, though I'm not sure how she can do that. Then I'll be the one to contact her. While I don't have her contact information, I know who she is. She helped secure the use of Max's lab for New-Bio. The way Max talks…um…talked, he and Carla had known each other a long time. Went to school together, I think, and even worked together at one point. She obviously felt close enough to Max to talk about these discrepancies she was seeing, and she might agree to talk to me."

"I hear you, Kinsley, and while you're probably right, she's going to be skittish. Wary about talking to anyone, especially after Max's death. She might also be monitored. If they killed Max for this information, and Carla is still alive, then one has to wonder why. Why wasn't she targeted. We'll need to be careful."

Just when he thought things couldn't get more dangerous...

"I agree this needs to be handled with nitrile exams gloves."

As opposed to "kid gloves." He smiled at her little joke but said nothing because he could tell she wasn't finished. She stared at the emails and then slowly turned to look at him.

Her blue-green eyes grew wide. "Thank you, Brett. I've been staring at this for hours, but I was so sure the answers would be found in the data he collected that I failed to even consider the emails. I'm not thinking all that clearly and two sets of eyes are better than one. I don't know what I would do without you." Her last words had come out breathy.

Heat surged from his heart. Heat and memories of how much he had loved this woman filled his mind. How much he still cared. She was everything he ever wanted—kind, caring, smart, compassionate, and the vanilla scent of her hair drove him crazy. Her lids dropped so that her eyes were partially hooded, and her lips parted, just so.

And he wanted to kiss her...

Heart pounding, Brett leaned in, against his better judgment. But he was powerless against her pull.

She suddenly pushed away from the table and

left him sitting there. He closed his eyes and took a few calming breaths to slow his pounding heart. Wrong time. Wrong place. What had he been thinking?

Good job, Brett. Way to make this even more awkward.

He stood too and turned. "Kinsley, wait. I'm sorry."

Where had she gone? The back door was partially opened. She'd turned off the alarm to leave. To get away from him. He couldn't let her stew out there alone. He needed to apologize, and then she could be mad at him only inside where it was safe and warm.

"Kinsley?" He walked around the house, then found her leaning against a porch post staring at the full moon.

Snowcapped Mt. Rainier practically glowed in the moonlight.

"Isn't the volcano incredible?" she whispered.

Had she already forgotten they had almost shared a kiss? He doubted it, but what a great distraction.

"Yes. It's gorgeous. I love living in the Pacific Northwest. It has everything. Mountains and valleys, rocky coasts with sea stacks. Flat shores to walk for miles. Islands and a rainforest. And my family is all here now."

Kinsley shivered and wrapped her arms

around herself. It might reach the high sixties during the day, but it was a cool low forties tonight. He reached for her, and she didn't resist as he wrapped his arms around her. Facing the moon, she leaned against *him* instead of the post. Kinsley seemed to have recovered from his mistake—his almost kiss.

Brett didn't want to say anything to ruin the moment. But maybe he should. Especially after she relaxed into him and sighed as if content.

If only he could trust himself to be the man she deserved.

SEVENTEEN

The next day at noon, in brand-new disguises, they leaned over their tacos at a food truck across the street from the NewBio campus. Kinsley's palms were sweating as she sat across from Brett at the small outdoor table.

"I feel like we're walking right into the lion's den," she said.

"Or the dragon's lair," he added. "But in either case, we've already walked in and are eating tacos."

Carla had told them that she often walked to the taco truck for lunch to get fresh air. She didn't want to change up her habits and draw attention, so she had agreed to meet them here today. She claimed she was walking on a precipice and couldn't leave or hide, so it was better to remain in plain sight.

In her peripheral vision, Kinsley watched the fifty-something woman with short blond hair and glasses order her tacos at the truck. She conversed with the man behind the counter and shared a laugh. It was obvious she frequented the place. In fact, he handed over her meal in record time.

"Brett," Kinsley whispered. "I think that's her."

"Remember what she said. Don't look at her. Look at me. Talk and laugh or something."

"I can't fake a laugh. Say something funny."

"How about a serious conversation instead. That would make more sense, considering we're about to get into a serious conversation with Carla."

"Okay. Sure. What can we talk about until she takes a seat close to us?" She already had her food.

Kinsley kept hoping that guy at the table next to them would hurry up and leave. Carla was supposed to sit next to them and eat. She'd told them she always sat at the table on the far right side, and they should grab the one next to that, and when she sat, they should already be at their table. They could talk without appearing to be talking. She would have an earbud in and her cell phone on the table and act like she was taking a phone call. Whatever happened, they could not be seen together.

God, please make us invisible.

Kinsley tugged her Seattle Seahawks gimme

cap lower. Brett wore a beanie and sunglasses. No one would expect them to be out in the open near NewBio, not even the notorious Lee Jackson. At least, she hoped not.

The nerdy tall dark-haired guy at the table next to them finally got up, and Carla slid into a chair across from them. As planned, she got her cell out and acted like she was making a call, plugged in her earbuds and opened her package of tacos. She never once looked at Kinsley or Brett. Kinsley hadn't looked either, but she watched the woman, again, with her peripheral vision.

"What do you want from me?" Carla asked, smiling as if she was talking to a friend.

She would be fine as long as no one actually listened to her words.

"We need help to get inside. I want justice for Max."

"I want that too, but I'm not going to help you get inside."

"I need to get my hands on the evidence."

"You don't need to get inside, because I'm already there."

Oh. Right. "Then why haven't you done anything about what's going on? Why don't you go to the police?"

"I'm scared."

Can't imagine why.

"I should have been targeted along with Max," she said.

"Unless he was targeted for a different reason," Brett said to Kinsley and took a bite of his taco as if this was just another day. Just another conversation.

"I can't imagine what that reason would be." Carla laughed like she'd heard the funniest joke, then squeezed salsa from a packet onto her taco.

Kinsley shared a look with Brett. Neither of them had imagined this scenario either. How could they know there wasn't yet another reason out there for which Max had been murdered and Kinsley targeted along with him? If this had to do with NewBio ethics, then why murder Max and not Carla? Why include Kinsley when she knew nothing about it?

"More than that, I'm afraid to quit or resign or try to hide. I know too much, and any attempt on my part to step out of line could trigger a kill shot. As for Kinsley, since she worked closely with Max, they suspect she knows what he knew."

Wow. "You can't live like this," Brett said.

"I can survive as long as it takes. The truth will come out. And now that you're here, I can breathe a little easier."

"What? Why?"

"I brought with me all the information you

could possibly need to bring down NewBio. I'll leave it in a taco wrapping on the table. You could act like you're cleaning up after me. Guard it with your life."

"Who can we give it to, Carla? Do you know everyone who is involved?"

"It's all in the information I'm giving to you. Until it comes out and people are arrested, our lives are still in danger. Please don't make me regret trusting you with this. I thought about ignoring your request. But when I heard your voice, I was so relieved to hear from you, and I knew it was time to take action. I don't know who I can trust with the police, so please be careful with this information."

Gunfire erupted. People screamed.

And Carla collapsed against the table.

Brett sprang forward and shoved Kinsley to the ground, then quickly urged her behind a tree. His heart jackhammered.

"Brett, Carla's hurt!"

She was more than hurt. She was dead. He'd seen her lifeless eyes. Brett couldn't believe someone had actually turned to this kind of violence and in the middle of the day with so many others around. Someone was getting desperate, and obviously knew Carla held damaging evidence.

He feared he and Kinsley would also be gunned down. He covered Kinsley with his body, but they needed to get moving as soon as he was sure they wouldn't be shot. "Stay here," he said. "I need to get the evidence that she gathered for us. Her life can't be for nothing. We have to end this."

"Brett, wait. They're watching and waiting for you to step into their gun sights. You can't. You'll be shot! And even if they don't shoot you, everyone here will see you. Everyone will think you're somehow involved in Carla's death."

Aren't I? After all, he'd gotten Everly to find the woman's contact information, and he and Kinsley had arranged to meet her. They had brought death to her, even if it had been inadvertent. He didn't have time to unpack it all.

He growled under his breath. "Just stay here. I'll be back and get you out of here."

Sirens rang out. The police were coming. He thought the shooters might be gone by then— but on the other hand, they could be waiting around for him to move from behind the tree. Without that evidence for which Carla had given her life, he and Kinsley were as good as dead too. It was the only way to end it.

He raced to the table, then snatched the taco wrapping that Carla had been good enough to fold around a thumb drive before she'd been killed. Brett hit the asphalt when more bullets pelted the table. He crawled over behind the food truck for some shelter. More screams erupted from those who'd already tried to hide behind the truck or other trees along with him.

He needed to make it back to Kinsley, who remained on the other side of the table where they'd been sitting. From behind the food truck, he stared at Kinsley, her blue-green eyes pinning him in place.

Lord, how do we get out of this?

Police arriving on the scene might save the day under normal circumstances. But for all he knew the dirty cop connection within the PD was in the police cruiser steering down the road toward them. Maybe the cop would even choose to finish the job. As the cruiser approached and people began to flee, Brett spotted a a man with a rifle racing away from behind a tree.

Now was his chance. He sprinted for Kinsley and grabbed her hand. Together they raced away from the scene and he pulled her into the gathering crowd to blend in even as he and Kinsley slowly inched their way to the back of the crowd. The scene had been so chaotic and terrifying that no one had paid them any attention, for which he was grateful.

He pulled out his cell and called Everly, talking to her as discreetly as he could as he and

Kinsley walked through a shopping strip, heading away from the shooting scene. "We need an egress. Taking the original vehicle is no longer an option."

"The news is talking about an active shooter at NewBio. You got out of there?"

"Yes. But we need to get *way* out of here before they set up a perimeter to stop the shooter from escaping. We both know who they are wanting to catch in that net."

"I can't help you," she said. "But I know someone who can. I've already been talking to Sawyer."

Sawyer Blackwood—Everly's fiancé. Of course, she would tell him. Brett should have expected it. Sawyer wasn't part of HPS and was a safe distance from the police, so their inside man—the dirty cop—might not have a read on him like he would HPS.

"I'm sorry. I really am. But I suspected you would need additional help, and I have too many eyes on me. Sawyer has connections and he lives under the radar of the usual authorities. I… I already took the liberty of having him secure you a vehicle—just in case. You'll need to walk five blocks east to the corner of Wells and James. Can you make it?"

"We'll have to. But Everly, how do you do it? How do you anticipate what people will need?"

"You're my brother. I want to make sure I cover every base. I know it's a matter of life and death. It stands to reason that you might need a different escape if things went south."

"When this is over—"

"You owe me nothing, Brett. Just survive."

He ended the call and turned back to Kinsley. "We need to walk five blocks. So let's get to it. The longer we're out in the open the more chances we'll have of being recognized." And killed.

Kinsley caught up to him. "Why five blocks?"

"Everly has a car waiting there for us. But we still need to hurry. They could block the radius around NewBio."

"I doubt they'll try. After all, there's still someone out there with a sniper rifle, and they don't want one of their own caught," she said.

"The police department is a group of great heroes, working for the people, Kinsley. Just because there's one bad apple in the group, doesn't make the whole batch bad, no matter what that old saying says. But until we know who it is, we don't know who to trust."

She slowed to catch her breath and he slowed with her. Wrapped his arm around her. "I think we should walk leisurely now, so we don't look like we're on a mad flight to escape."

"Sounds good to me. I just want to hurry so

we can find out what is in that information Carla collected. I want to know who killed Max. And then…what, Brett? Are we going to bring this Lincoln person in? How do you know he isn't the bad guy?"

I don't.

As they passed an electronic store, Brett spotted the newsfeed on the scene and a replay someone had captured on their cell phone. It was playing across the big-screen televisions. His face was all over the television as he scraped the taco wrapper off Carla's table, appearing to have no regard for the dead woman.

I'm in trouble.

EIGHTEEN

Back at the safe house, Kinsley breathed a sigh of relief when Brett shut the door behind them. "How long do you think it'll be before they find us?"

"I think we're out of time." He moved to the table and opened the laptop. "If Carla encrypted that drive, I don't know if Everly can help us now. But we need to look at it. Then we're going to contact HPS to handle our protection and the delivery of the evidence to the authorities."

She closed the distance. "You think we'll find out who the connection is in the PD? That would go a long way in making it easier for me to come out of hiding and trust the police to take things from here."

"Let's hope so." The dark look in Brett's eyes didn't reassure her.

She understood. The heaviness, the grief, weighed on her too. Carla had survived this long and had died handing over this evidence to them. They had to get justice for both her and Max.

Brett remained standing as he pulled out the chair. For her? "No. You sit," she said. "You look at the evidence. I'll be right here, looking over your shoulder."

His expression remaining grim, he nodded and sat. He booted up the laptop and stuck in the thumb drive. The files came right up, and Kinsley released another breath. "At least we're in, and don't need someone to hack into it for us."

"Carla wanted us to have access and know what was going on," he pointed out. "Why make it more difficult than it already was to get to the point where we can learn the truth? I just wish she would have agreed to meet in another place. A safe place. Maybe we should the tried harder to convince her to go into hiding after stashing the information somewhere for us to pick up. Maybe if we had, she would still be alive."

"Don't blame yourself, Brett. It was her choice. You did everything you could."

"We did everything we could, Kinsley. You insisted on being the one to contact her and I don't think she would have agreed to talk or meet otherwise."

Brett focused on the files. Together they read through the documents as he opened them. Carla outlined original clinical trial results, compared to published trial results, all signed off by a man named Hector Wallis—the Director of Clinical Drug Development at NewBio.

Nausea erupted. Kinsley stepped back.

Brett suddenly jumped up and turned to her. Grabbed her. "Kinsley, what is it? Are you okay?"

She reached for her throat. *I can't breathe.*

Brett gently shook her. "Kinsley, talk to me. Take a deep breath."

"The voice I heard that night over the cell. It sounded familiar but I couldn't place it. Now I know who it belonged to. Hector Wallis—I met him once when he showed up for a tour of the lab. Every six months, Max attends a teleconference. I heard his voice there, too. Seeing his face now jogged my memory."

Kinsley closed her eyes and took more calming breaths. When she opened them, Brett was still looking at her with concern. Still holding her arms. He slowly released her.

"Are you sure about this?" He arched a brow. "It sounds like it has been a while since you heard his voice."

"I'm certain."

"Would it help if we found a video clip of him talking?"

"No. I knew the voice sounded familiar, Brett, I just couldn't place it. But now I can. It's him." Kinsley dragged in a ragged breath. Still stunned at the news. "Why would he want to kill someone? I can't fathom the murder over... what? Data? I know we've been searching for this exact kind of information all along but now that we've found it, I'm so angry that Max was murdered, and I was meant to die too."

"Max and Carla were obviously building a case." Brett's tone was calm and measured. "But there could be more. Let's keep reading the information. Okay?"

She nodded. "I'm good. Let's do it."

She joined him at the table again. Next to him, she felt safe and secure. He'd come through for her in a big way. She hadn't expected things to go this far. But they were still in it, and she focused on the screen once again, pulling up a chair to sit closer.

"Wait, there's an email from Max to Carla," she said. "I wonder why we didn't see this one in *his* files?"

"I'll open it. Let's find out."

Thanks for your help, Carla. He needs to pay for his crimes. Unfortunately none of this helps me prove that he murdered my best friend and his wife, Kinsley's parents. He's arrogant and self-absorbed. The only life he cares about is his own. If I can take him down by proving his unethical practices, then that's what I'll do.

Pulse roaring in her ears, Kinsley leaned closer and read it again. Her heart might have stopped.

"Kinsley." Brett pulled her in his arms. "I'm so so sorry, honey."

"Max never told me any of this. I thought... I thought it was a car accident!"

Sobbing in anger and rekindled grief, she moved away from Brett and ran through the house. Out the back door into the cold rain.

God, why?

Her parents had worked hard to save others. Why had this happened to them? *How* could this have happened? Brett caught up to her and pulled her back out of the rain onto the porch and into his sturdy arms. Racking sobs flooded out of her and into his sturdy chest. His arms around her were strong and protective and his voice comforting. After a few moments when her tears were finally spent, she looked up into his caring, handsome face. Light from the window illuminated his features.

Tenderness rushed through her. She was vulnerable and raw and maybe that allowed her to see what she hadn't wanted to see. In Brett's eyes, she saw the man she'd known years ago. The man she'd loved.

Kinsley stood on her tiptoes to kiss him, but she soon dropped flat on her feet as he leaned in and returned her kiss. Her heart flooded with warmth that filled the emptiness.

Brett eased away but his lips were still pressed lightly against hers. Would he apologize again? She slowly stepped away. "Brett…"

I knew this was a bad idea.

Don't forget. The man standing here, kissing her back, was the Brett she'd loved before.

And that Brett had hurt her . Since he still needed therapy to move beyond what troubled him, he could very well stomp on her heart again.

Brett's heart ached at the look in Kinsey's eyes. He shouldn't have kissed her, but neither could he reject her when she'd been the one to kiss him. Either action seemed to be the wrong move. She was vulnerable and raw and probably hadn't truly meant to kiss him.

What do I say in this moment?

Anything he said would hurt her. Would hurt them both.

Kinsley suddenly shrugged away. Her expression told him he'd somehow *already* hurt her, without even saying a word.

She stomped back into the house. This just kept getting better and better. He needed to work this out with Kinsley, but even if he didn't, and things remained awkward between them, personally, at least they had some evidence, though they still didn't know who all the culprits were. He would try to focus on that, because that was why he was here, after all—not to get back together with Kinsley.

He followed her inside and shut the door. He wouldn't even try to apologize or address the kiss. "Now's the time to bring in HPS officially, Kinsley. We need all hands on deck to protect us through this next phase. You understand that, right?"

Her blue-green eyes still shimmered with emotions—regret and pain. He couldn't be sure which of that was from the kiss he'd allowed, or from the news she'd learned.

She stared at him. He'd wanted to earn her trust before it came to bringing in HPS.

"We still don't know who the dirty cop is," she said.

Her tone had some bite to it. He would ignore it. "Maybe not, but the pieces will begin to fall into place soon enough once Hector is exposed."

"Will it? He'll just hire high-powered lawyers, and nothing will change. Meanwhile, Max's and Carla's murders, my parents' murders, will remain unsolved."

"I agree we need to tie the murders to Hector, but that's just further proof that we're in over our heads and need more help. We have a certain amount of truth now, but we can't go any further with this on our own." Please, understand."

Kinsley appeared skittish, as if she might run from him. He took a timid step forward and held his hands out. "I didn't want to do this without your agreement." *I want you to trust me.* But if he told her that, she could very well see that as an ulterior motive to his actions.

She hugged herself. "Okay. Sure. Call them. Make arrangements. I have a pounding headache. Do you care if I lie down for a while?"

"That's a good idea. But please remain ready to jump and leave. We might need a fast escape. I don't want to stay here tonight so I'm working on plans for another safe location."

Pursing her lips, she nodded and disappeared down the hallway.

Brett released a heavy exhale. That Carla had been killed right before their eyes had been traumatizing for them both, but adding in that Max had been trying to bring Hector down for killing Kinsley's parents… It was no wonder she had been pushed over the edge. Brett would like to know the rest of the story and see the proof Max had, but if her parents knew that Hector was pushing drugs that could harm rather than heal, maybe that was enough reason to kill them— just like he killed Max.

Kinsley could testify she'd heard Hector's voice. Her testimony could take him down.

She was still very much in danger.

He stared at his cell. Everly was supposed to contact him, using an untraceable phone she had secured, and he didn't have that number yet. He couldn't call her on her regular cell because that might lead the wrong people to this location.

Brett sat back at the laptop and continued skimming through the notes and information that Carla had provided. He also uploaded the information to a private file storage on the cloud, in case something happened to the thumb drive, and included documentation of the evidence trail. As he worked, he tried not to think about kissing Kinsley. What kind of jerk would kiss someone when they were in such a bad place, taking advantage of them? But the emotions had been raw on both sides.

And they were still raw. His heart ached for what she was going through. Ached for missing her in his arms. He was a selfish jerk. And he needed to build up a wall again and keep his distance. That was the least he could do to protect her from a man like him, who could only ever hurt her again.

How could he want her to trust him when he didn't even trust himself?

His cell rang and he stared at the number. It

could be a wrong number. Or it could be Everly. He answered the call but said nothing.

"It's me. Sawyer and Lincoln are on their way to your location."

"Good. We're ready to fully come in now."

"I thought you would be. Better us than someone else."

"I loaded the files Carla gave us onto our private cloud storage so you could access them."

"I'm looking at them now and transferring them to additional locations. There's a lot of evidence here."

"But Kinsley is still the key witness to connect Hector to Max's murder," he said, concern for her building in his chest. "She recognized his voice that night at the lab explosion."

"Oh. I didn't know that piece of the puzzle."

"Sorry I didn't lead with it."

"We still don't know who his connection is within the PD, but with Hector's name, I can now begin digging and find out who he knows in the department. The connection won't be random. As for Lee Jackson, he doesn't show up in any criminal databases or even military. We're running facial recognition software on him and will let you know when we get a hit."

Lights shined in the windows. "Someone's outside."

"I just got a text from Sawyer. It's them. He wants to know where you are."

"What do you mean? I'm here. Did you send them to the wrong location?"

"Hold on."

He could hear Everly typing a text.

"He responded, saying that the lights are on at the house but the car is gone."

Brett sprang from the table and ran to the room where Kinsley had gone to sleep. She wasn't there. He raced to the front door and threw it open, then ran outside as Sawyer and Lincoln got out of their vehicle.

"Kinsley's gone." His words came out breathless. *How could she do this?*

"Gone?" Sawyer asked.

"What happened?" Lincoln closed the distance, his brows furrowed.

No one was as shocked as he was. No one was angrier. "She said she was going to lie down. I didn't hear her leave. What have I done?"

"Just calm down." Sawyer spoke in an even tone. "Where could she have gone?"

"We…we just learned that not only is Hector Wallis behind Max's death, but Max believed that Wallis killed her parents, too. That's why Max had set out to take him down."

"You think she's going to try something on her own?"

"It's possible. The idea she ran by me earlier was to break into NewBio."

"What?" Lincoln said a few more choice words. "This is making her look guiltier."

"She's not guilty and to my eyes, this is making her look desperate to clear her name."

"Do you think she is going to try to break into NewBio then?" Sawyer stayed on topic.

"She doesn't have the skill set. She'd need some help to do it—she's sharp enough to know that."

"Then where'd she make off to, that she didn't feel she could bring you?"

Brett paced in a small circle. "She's furious with Hector and can't see beyond the fact he might have murdered her parents. We don't even know it's true. We don't know why Max believed that. So what if she is on her way to Wallis's home to face off with him? If it was me, I would probably do the same thing."

He closed his eyes and sent up a silent prayer. *God, please protect her.*

Because she was stepping into a death trap.

NINETEEN

What am I doing, what am I doing, what am I doing?

"I'm so sorry, Brett." Kinsley steered along the posh neighborhood road.

She wished she could have included him in this plan, but he wouldn't have agreed to it. Kinsley was taking a huge risk, but she couldn't let Hector get away with murder again. He'd already gotten away with murdering her parents. Then Max and now Carla. She and Brett were taking far too long to get answers. Kinsley was willing to go all the way with this to prevent this murderer from winning, from killing anyone else.

After losing everyone dear to her, Kinsley didn't care about anything—even her own safety—except looking him in the eyes.

She'd get his confession, record it on the cell she had. Because Max had provided no proof, and Hector's high-powered lawyers would get him off on a technicality or claim someone had forged his signature on documents. The two people who knew the most about Hector's unethical practices were dead. She strongly suspected the other microbiologists and scientists behind producing the false reports would also be taken out or hidden away if she were to try to find them. Maybe they were already gone from NewBio if not this world.

Kinsley parked down the street from Hector's address. The large estate could only be entered through a coded gate. She'd been thinking about how she would get inside the long drive and had a loose plan. She waited behind bushes near the gate and noted the direction of the cameras.

Vehicle lights shined along the road and turned up the drive. She hunkered deeper into the shadows. The vehicle slowed and then stopped at the gate keypad. Now! Kinsley rushed across the drive behind the vehicle, staying out of the camera's view and the driver's mirrors as best she could.

Her heart hammered against her rib cage.

I must have lost my mind.

But the loss of life, the lies, would stop tonight.

Hector was going to pay, and this would probably be her only chance to face off with him, one-on-one. Even after Brett presented the evidence, it could be days or weeks before the evidence was corroborated and Hector and NewBio were investigated—assuming he wasn't able to use his influence to get the investigation held up.

He might even leave the country.

The gates creaked open, and the vehicle slowly pulled through them. Crouching, Kinsley kept near as it was driven onto the property. Once the vehicle cleared the gate and was inside, she dove into the bushes along the wall on the other side. She'd have to remember to thank the landscaper for unintentionally providing cover.

Though he had a gate for privacy, Hector probably never considered someone might actually try to break into his property. Kinsley took a moment to catch her breath and think through the next part of her plan. She moved in the shadows from tree to tree, and when she was in the shadows near the house, she waited and watched for a possible entry point. The house remained mostly in darkness except for a few rooms. She'd learned as much as she could about Hector before making this decision, taking these actions, before even leaving the safe house.

Hector was divorced with no children and lived alone, as far as she could tell.

The vehicle she'd followed in parked on the circular drive in front of the house. A woman slipped out the front door and into the vehicle. Then it left the premises.

Kinsley made her way around to the back of the house and watched for security guards or anyone else who might be around. She could see inside the home and spotted Hector sitting at his desk in a big posh office. The house had several doors, including a side door and a kitchen door. And then French doors. With the woman slipping out, maybe the alarm system hadn't been set yet.

Kinsley had suffered too much loss already, and this was a risk she was willing to take to make things right and to get justice for Max and her parents. This was what she had to do to look the man who killed her parents in the eyes. Approaching the French doors at the back, she could easily see into the house. Sudden movement caught her attention, and she dove behind bushes again.

Hector stepped outside and pulled his cell out. He made a call that went to voice mail, then grumbled without leaving a message. He paced. Now was the moment she could face him. But her heart jumped to her throat and her palms grew moist. He turned and entered the house again.

What am I doing? This was my chance. After her heart rate slowed, she stood from the bushes. She could hear his voice on the phone from his office. Or…wait…through the French doors. He'd failed to close them completely. She'd never get a better opportunity.

It's now or never.

She crept through the house, her cell phone turned on and the recording app on along with an additional fail-safe. Light spilled through the open door of his office. She slowly entered and stood there a few seconds. Hector sat behind his mahogany executive desk, frowning at his cell that rested in the center. Did she want to continue with her plan? Or slip out of the house and get away before she took this next step? He hadn't seen her yet. She could still walk away.

Then his head came up sharply and eyes widened. "Who are you? How did you get in here?"

"Why did you kill my parents?"

His eyes narrowed… "I'll ask again. Who are you?"

"You don't recognize me? You tried to kill me."

"I don't know what you're talking about. I'm calling the police."

He wasn't responding the way she'd expected. He was acting like he didn't even know her. But then, what had she expected? He must be a smart man to have gotten where he was. If only she had a gun, he might be more willing to talk. But Kinsley wasn't going to kill him. She only wanted a confession. He was arrogant and self-important. She could work with that.

Kinsley moved to the desk and seized the cell from his hand. She'd had the advantage in that he hadn't expected her to move so aggressively, but he wouldn't be fooled a second time.

"I'm Kinsley Langell. You know who I am. Stop playing dumb. You want me dead. You're going to kill me, remember? Before I die, I want to know why you killed my parents."

Come on, take the bait.

"Kinsley?" He slowly sighed. "I guess I at least owe you that much." He closed his eyes as if remembering or measuring his words. Then opened them to look at her. "Your father and I worked together, early in our careers. Did you know that? Long before he worked with Max. We stayed in touch even when we went our separate ways—him overseas with Doctors Without Borders, and me continuing to build my career in pharmaceutical development. Your mother and I were engaged."

"What? That's not true."

"It's true, all right. Your father stole her from me. What could I say? She chose *him* over me."

"Well if it was her choice, then he didn't steal her."

"No matter. When they started interfering with my work and ran the risk of setting me back decades…well, I couldn't let that continue. I couldn't trust them to stop interfering."

"How exactly did they interfere?"

His eyes narrowed. "I see what's happening here. You want a confession. Thinking you're going to get out of here alive."

"Don't even think about standing up from that chair. You underestimate me. If you get up, cyanogen bromide will be released. A long time ago you actually worked in a lab. Maybe you remember what that will do to you? No? Let me remind you. Even if you don't breathe it in, your skin will absorb it. It's acutely toxic and will kill you. I'll step out of the office and close the door the moment you stand. It won't touch me. But you won't have time to escape."

She tried to keep from shaking as she said the words. She could never kill another person. Even a murderer like Hector. But she could bluff if it meant getting what she needed.

Hector laughed and waved his hand. "You're not a killer, Kinsley. You save lives."

Hector acted like he thought she was bluffing , but he was too. He hadn't moved from the chair.

Good.

He couldn't take the risk that she was telling the truth.

"Believe it or not, that's all I want to do, too,"

he continued. "I want to save lives. But if someone tries to get in the way of that, then they pay
the price. I believe the means justifies the end."

"You're a monster."

"Don't you get it? There are a lot of pharma-
ceuticals that could already be on the market
helping people, if not for government oversight
and regulations. Too much red tape—that's
what is costing lives."

Her time was up, and she'd gotten the recording she'd wanted. She would leave him sitting
in the chair and get out of here, get into the vehicle then head back to the safe house or call
Everly or Brett. She had gotten the evidence
they needed.

She fully expected that Brett would have discovered her missing by now, called either Everly
or the police to track and follow her vehicle and
find Kinsley. Show up and save the day.

But her time had run out, and it seemed no
one was here.

The muzzle of a gun pressed against the base
of her skull.

A man stepped around and she recognized
him as one of the saboteurs at the lab. Her whole
body shook but she lifted her chin in defiance.
Another man rushed into the room. He knelt on
the floor beneath Hector's chair, and then stood,
shaking his head. "She was bluffing."

Hector stood. He lifted his chin as if signaling to someone behind her.

She felt a prick to her skin. Wooziness rushed through her as she lost control of her limbs and collapsed. She glanced up to blurry images hovering above her before everything went dark.

A whimpering noise broke into her dreams, like the sound a puppy would make. Her head pounded. Kinsley's whole body ached. Memories flooded back to her, and fear gripped her. Blinking, she opened her eyes to bright light, creeping in between the bars. She tried to lift her head, but she was crammed into a too small cage, curled up on her side.

And the whimpering? She glanced to the side. A small mutt in the cage next to her with big brown sad eyes cried out.

Oh, no!

They'd brought her to the experimental lab filled with animals where they tested various drugs. Tools of the trade—machines, syringes, blood vials, brushes and funnels, sieves and stirring rods—were organized on a nearby table. It seemed that she was in a cage until they decided what to do with her.

Hector was toying with her. Enjoying this entirely too much.

She'd risked everything in going to his house,

but he'd confessed. She'd gotten it on her cell. Unless…

She felt around in her pockets, but her cell was gone. No matter, she'd called a recording service, and everything that was said had been recorded off-site. Max used to send notes to the service that would record his notes and a person would transcribe them. And in the end, she'd gotten that confession—though she'd risked her life to get it. It was no less than what Carla had done in meeting them and transferring evidence to them.

Brett would never have agreed to her methods.

But she almost wanted to pump her fist because it had worked.

Unfortunately, she didn't have enough room to pump her fist. Why, if they were going to put her in a cage, did it have to be so small? Then again, in looking around the lab, she saw this was actually the largest cage. A door opened and closed and the rabbits, hamsters, guinea pigs and dogs started whimpering, crying and barking. Kinsley shuddered and tears surged. What a horrible place this was. She understood that suitable nonanimal methods hadn't been created for testing and that there were no perfect answers—but there had to be a better option than this. If she got out of this, she would need to make an effort to adopt a lab animal.

Keys jangled and someone entered the lab, pushing a table. No, wait. A bed. Was that straps hanging off it?

Oh, no, no, no. Maybe that wasn't for her and whoever had entered didn't even know she was a captive here. He did something she couldn't make out. Too many cages, animals, and that table stood in the way. She angled her head just right and caught him setting a syringe on the edge of the table, near the bed.

So—this *was* for her.

She would not be taken again.

I was such a fool to take this risk.

She was a fool to believe that Brett would find her and save the day. It wasn't his fault, though. It was completely on her. Someone approached the cage, and she waited in fear until his face came into view.

Lee Jackson.

He bent down and smirked at her in the cage. "You'll get a treat if you continue to be a good girl."

Oh. Boy. If she got out of here, he was going to pay. Her mind raced with possible scenarios. None of them ended well for her.

"What are you going to do with me?" she asked.

"Wouldn't you like to know." It was a statement rather than a question.

Actually, getting out of the experimental lab would be an improvement. Lee opened the lock, then swung the cage wide. He pointed a gun at her. She scrambled out and stretched to get the kinks out of her body, then looked at him with her own smirk.

"How's your head?" she asked.

He scowled. "You don't know what you've gotten into."

"Why don't you tell me?" She would not cooperate. The longer she could drag this out the better.

Maybe Brett hadn't found her at Hector's, but she had no doubt he was looking.

He would move heaven and earth to find her, if he could.

God, please let him move heaven and earth to find me.

"I don't think I will," Lee said. "Walk on."

He gestured for her to go ahead of him. Did he know she'd already learned most of the truth? Did *he* even know—or care about—the truth?

She strolled slowly, then pretended to trip and knocked vials and tubes off the table for cover as she reached for the one she wanted. Then she fell flat on her back, as if unconscious.

"Well that's just wonderful. Get up and stop jerking me around."

He kicked her. Kinsley moaned but didn't open her eyes.

Come and get me, jerk.

Lee got a call on his cell. "Yeah. I got her ready."

He ended the call and said a few choice words. From what she could hear, they were expecting him to have her sedated and on the table. She didn't want to know what Hector had planned for her. Lee bent down and grabbed her. She injected the syringe into his arm as he stared on with a look of horror. He lifted the gun, but she knocked it out of his hand. The drug must have kicked in because he collapsed against her, grunting. It took some effort but adrenaline rushed through her and she rolled the big man off her, and scrambled to her feet. Kinsley gasped for breath. Did that really happen?

She had no time to think and instead took action. Moving to each cage, she opened them to free the animals. Then she raced to the door but found it locked.

She glanced up at the camera.

Oh, no. She searched Lee for a key or a passcard and found nothing on him. She'd have to find another way out.

Kinsley rushed to the table and found flammable chemicals, combined them, and soaked a cloth, then turned on the Bunsen burner to produce a flame. The rag caught on fire immediately, and she placed it directly under the sprinklers that were required in all facilities. She made sure nothing was near the burning rag on the table and that it would burn itself out— but not before she got the results she wanted.

The smoke alarms blared, water rained down from the ceiling... And the door automatically opened.

She dashed out. Animals scurried everywhere. She had no idea how to get out of here and could only hope that the animals would start enough chaos that no one would be able to find her quickly. Was she in a basement floor? She found a stairwell, then started up.

She hoped firefighters would soon be here. Kinsley raced down the main hallway toward the exits. Security lights from outside drew her forward. She sprinted toward the exit. *Please, God, let me get out of here!*

Suddenly Brett was there—just outside the glass doors, searching. He raced toward the building. She'd never been so glad to see anyone.

So glad to see Brett.

If she made it out of here, she would jump into his arms.

I don't care if it's a risk to love him.

TWENTY

Brett raced to the glass doors. He could hardly believe that Kinsley was running toward him. He hadn't been certain he would find her here. No one had been at the Wallis premises.

And as he ran, all he could think about was getting her out of here and somewhere safe. More than that, he wanted to pull her into his arms and kiss her again. If he had to spend the rest of his life proving to her, and to himself, that he was the man for her, he would do it. He only needed her to give him another chance. To give *them* a chance. He couldn't be an idiot again and let her go.

But coming to NewBio—Why had she risked so much?

Brett got to the door, but it was locked. Kinsley wasn't to the door yet, but maybe she would be able to push it open from inside.

Suddenly, from behind Kinsley, a man rushed out from a side door—Hector Wallis—and wrapped his arm around her throat. He pressed a gun to her head and dragged her back and away from the door.

Brett slammed his fists against the glass doors. Kinsley screamed and kicked, but Hector slammed the gun into the side of her head. Dazed, she went limp as he continued to drag her along. He tossed Brett a smug look as he took Kinsley.

What? "Stop it. Hector. Let her go!" Brett banged on the glass door, feeling helpless to stop Wallis. "Leave her alone. You'll never get away with this. What are you doing? What do you want?"

Brett backed up and aimed his Glock at the doors. Heart pounding, Brett wanted to blast a hole through the glass if that was what it took to gain entrance. But he couldn't risk shooting Kinsley. Or having Hector shoot her. Pressing his face against the glass so he could see in the darkened hallways, he spotted the man taking the elevators. He suddenly realized there were no security guards inside the building. How strange... Or were they all working for Wallis in this devious plan, judiciously turning a blind eye?

Brett called Everly and she answered quickly. Breathless, he tried to explain. "Everly, he got her. He took her."

"What?"

"Hector. I saw him at NewBio. He grabbed Kinsley and took her away at gunpoint."

"Oh, no. Brett. I'm on it. Just tell me what you want me to do."

"Bring everyone in," Brett said. "Caine and Ayden. Get Lincoln on it. Get S.W.A.T. The guy's abducting Kinsley. We can't let him take her."

"If he's in the building, he's not going to get far. I'm contacting the police right now. But you call 9-1-1 too."

"There's no time," he said. "I'm going inside. Hector's the man behind it all. He was the man behind everything. But my concern is we still don't know who his connection is in the P.D."

"Lincoln hasn't been able to discover that. I thought he and Sawyer were with you?"

"They're trying to get a warrant to get into Wallis's house."

"I'll let them know what's happening. You let me worry about that dirty cop, Brett. Now go get her."

He aimed his pistol at the doors. Then he heard the rotors of the helicopter heading toward the roof. Brett had to stop him, keep him from taking Kinsley.

Here goes nothing. Brett aimed his gun and shot holes through the glass door. He kicked it in, then raced for the elevator. He wouldn't make it if he took the stairs. He might not make it even if he took the elevator. But maybe Everly could delay things.

Inside the building, he called Everly again. "Helicopter on the roof. Everly, you have to stop him. Keep him from taking her. Hack into his helicopter. Do what you can. Track him at the very least."

"I'll do what I can. Listen, Brett, I've got some news."

Brett listened as he pressed elevator buttons until one finally opened for him. Brett got on and pressed the button to the top floor, surprised he didn't need a special key. The elevator moved much too slowly. But he'd heard some good news from Everly at the end of their call. Finally. Now to save Kinsley before it was too late.

Come on, come on, come on.

He paced inside the small box. *Think, Brett. Lord, please help me get there in time.*

All he needed was a small delay. He had to prepare in case he faced opposition, or he faced off with Hector holding a gun to Kinsley. He didn't want to find himself in an active hostage situation. He pressed the button to the floor just beneath the top floor.

He got off, then raced down the empty hallway and up the stairwell. On the last floor, he searched for a stairwell to the top of the building.

Well, look at that. There's a sign that directs people to the helipad. He quietly opened the door. Gun ready, he crept up the stairs where he could hear the rotor wash outside.

He peered through the small glass frame in the door and watched as a man forced Kinsley into the waiting helicopter.

The rotor wash, the jostling pushed through the grogginess and she suddenly became aware of what was happening around her. She felt her head and found a knot where Hector had hit her, dazing her.

Someone was forcing her into a helicopter.

I have to escape.

But she still couldn't get her limbs to cooperate.

"No. No, leave me alone. Let me go." Her leg kicked out, finally responding. Yes. Her body was functioning again. She landed punches in his midsection, but Hector was like a stone-cold wall. Nothing she did fazed him. He blocked her attempts to hit him in the face.

"Why are you doing this? If you abduct me, then you're only getting yourself into much more legal trouble."

"No one is going to know, Kinsley, don't you

get it? You're responsible for blowing up that lab. All the evidence is stacked against you."

He climbed in next to her, trapping her inside with him. Would he toss her body where it would never be found? But if that was his plan, why not kill her back at the house? Why bring her to the lab just to take her away in a helicopter? Why come to the lab at all? He was finally getting desperate. Maybe he wanted information from her, but she had the feeling that if he couldn't get it, he'd decide silencing her was more important and would dump her body.

And what about Brett? He'd seen Hector grab her. Would Hector kill Brett too? She elbowed him in the throat, stunning him for a moment, giving herself enough time to open the door. She tried to scramble out, but he recovered from her punch and snatched her, trying to pull her back inside with him. She struggled with everything she could muster, knowing she had to escape before the helicopter lifted off.

"Don't you get it? Too many people know about you already. You can't get away with it."

"I have connections."

"Not anymore you don't," Brett shouted. He aimed his gun at Hector's head.

"Detective Casey Rains has been arrested for tampering with evidence, and for plotting with you to kill Max Stevens and Kinsley Langell.

Detective Rains's brother, Lee Jackson, once he's found, will be arrested. Your henchmen lab conspirators—Jay Morris and Rod Willis—have been captured trying to flee. You have no one left to do your dirty work, Wallis."

Brett's words must have gotten to Hector. He briefly loosened his grip on Kinsley. It was enough for her to throw her head back and connect. She scrambled free and escaped the helicopter at last. Gunfire rang out and she dove behind a large air-conditioning unit. Brett raced for the helicopter as it lifted, and he tugged Hector out of it.

The two men fell a few feet and crashed on the concrete.

Hector landed multiple punches at Brett, who tried to block him. Then Hector started pistol-whipping him. Kinsley wanted to ram into him and break his connection, but she already knew the man spent time in a gym. And she also knew that Brett was strong and skilled, and he wouldn't be bested.

Brett suddenly broke free and landed a front kick in Hector's throat. Kinsley had hit him there once before in the helicopter, but Brett's kick must have done some real damage. The man fell back and grasped his neck, looking like he was choking. Gun aimed at his head, Brett stood over him.

Hector glared. The helicopter took off, but

Kinsley got the N-number, and she memorized the pilot's face. A SWAT team in full tactical gear and loaded for bear, rushed onto the roof. Police officers stepped through the fray.

Brett lifted his gun high over his head along with his hands and announced his identity, but it looked like they were going to arrest him too.

Kinsley lifted her hands and rushed forward. "He saved me. What are you doing? He saved me. Hector Wallis was trying to abduct me."

"She's lying." Hector had been lifted onto his feet now. He had a smirk on his face as he looked at her. "She conspired with this man to destroy the lab and kill Max Stevens."

Another man stepped forward, pushing his way through the law enforcement presence. "Hector Wallis? I'm Detective Lincoln Mann. You're under arrest." He nodded at another officer who cuffed Hector.

The detective stepped toward Brett and Kinsley. "We'll need you both to come in for questioning. We have a lot to sort out."

A woman rushed forward. Up to then, Kinsley had only seen her image on the computer. "Everly?"

"Yes!" Everly hugged Kinsley. "It's going to be okay. I've delivered all the evidence I could gather from the cloud." Everly gripped her shoulders and leveled her gaze. "Lincoln just needs to sort it all out. Okay? Just tell the truth. You were afraid to go to the police. Afraid for your life."

"I sent Hector's confession to a transcription service."

Everly smiled and arched a brow. "Really? I'm looking forward to getting to know you better."

Two days later, Kinsley woke up in a strange place. Again. But then she remembered she was sleeping at the Honor Protection Specialists headquarters. The room was comfortable but had no windows. Understandable since their facilities were used as a safe house at times. When she'd tried to go home, she'd discovered that it had been ransacked by Hector's men and so remained a crime scene. She'd had no place to go. Not really. But staying here was fine with her and allowed her to get some rest and try to process everything that had happened. Detective Mann had stopped by a few times to ask more questions.

Even Gil had checked in on a video-conferencing call just to see how she and Brett had fared.

She was the only witness to the lab conversation, after all, but her recording of Wallis's confession would go a long way in convicting him of multiple crimes. She'd been in school and had no idea that her parents had been trying to stop Hector from bringing what they believed was a dangerous drug to market—he'd been trying to force it through for years. Her parents continued to monitor him through their connections. . Hector knew of their efforts and had arranged for someone to T-bone them in a big truck.

Squeezing her eyes shut, she let the tears flow. She had answers to questions she hadn't known about only last week. Somehow, someway, she would have to keep moving. Put one foot in front of the other and carve out a new life, though she wasn't sure what she would do next. At least all Max's work—most of it—remained on the servers. It would take time to sort out what happened to the data and what big pharma company would take it on next. Certainly not NewBio. While she didn't know her future, she knew that she didn't want to move forward without Brett in her life. After everything, she wasn't afraid to take the risk of him hurting her. If she walked away now, she would always wonder what might have been. She only needed to know how he felt.

With that thought, she got out of bed and quickly showered and dressed. She hoped that Brett was still here and hadn't found a reason to disconnect from her completely. She opened the door and peered down the long hallway. Kinsley made her way down the hall toward the main offices, which included a kitchen. She peeked inside and saw Ayden and Caine and Everly talking over coffee.

Everly spotted her and turned her attention to Kinsley. "Good morning. Would you like some breakfast?"

"Maybe in a bit. Do you know where Brett is?"

"He left earlier this morning, but he'll be back."

Kinsley didn't want them to see her obvious disappointment, so she stepped out of the kitchen. Instead of heading to her room, she went into one of the main offices and looked out the window at Mt. Rainier, thinking back to that night they'd stood out in the cold and looked at the mountain. The other time, she'd kissed him in the cold rain, then rushed away from him because she'd been too afraid to love him again. Maybe she was making mistake. She should go to her room and pack her items. She needed to leave. Needed her own space.

Kinsley pressed her face into her hands.

"Kinsley?" Brett's voice sounded pained.

She turned to see him approaching from the front door. He looked like he'd been smiling but was now halfway between a smile and concern.

"What's wrong?" He joined her at the window, never taking his eyes from hers.

"I've taken advantage of this place too long. I should probably get going."

"What? No." He pressed his hands gently against her biceps. "Your place isn't released yet, and I… I like having you close."

"Do you?"

"Of course. Why wouldn't I?"

"What are we doing, Brett?"

He dug around in his pocket. Surely…no…he couldn't be. And then, to her surprise, he pulled out a small container of ash.

"Recognize this?"

"St. Helens ash."

"The place is beautiful now, even after the devastation. It reminds me of the Bible verse about beauty for ashes." He placed the small jar in her hand and wrapped his around it. "I burned the bridges between us years ago and turned our relationship to ash. I know that. But it can be beautiful once again, Kinsley, if you're willing to try. I'll get whatever help I need to get, but I know that I can only be better with you by my side. I love you. Will you give us a second chance? I know you're scared of being hurt. Honestly, I'm scared too—but I think the risk is worth it."

She lifted her hand to cup his cheek and felt the strength in his jaw, the stubble in his skin, and her love surged inside. "I never stopped loving you, and now I think I'm finally ready to take that risk with you again. We just have to take it one step at a time."

He flicked his gaze to the ash as if he wanted her to look too. She turned the small clear jar around to watch the ash glisten and then she spotted something inside. Her breath quickened. "Brett, what is that?"

"Open it up and see."

She opened the jar and stuck her fingers in and then drew out a ring. A ring? A solitaire diamond? She couldn't breathe. She held it but didn't know what to say.

"I know it feels soon, but I was going to ask you to marry me three years ago, when I returned from that mission, but it all got messed up." He took the ring from her and slid it on the appropriate finger. "We can take our time, Kinsley. If at any time this doesn't feel right on your finger, then you can take it off. But I wanted you to know my commitment to you."

Kinsley was too overcome to speak, but she lifted her face and he met her halfway, planting his lips on hers. Then she slipped her arms around his neck and let joy carry her away.

* * * * *

If you enjoyed Deadly Sabotage
by USA TODAY *bestselling
author Elizabeth Goddard
Then be sure to check out*
Perilous Security Detail!
Available now from Love Inspired Suspense.

Discover more at LoveInspired.com

Dear Reader,

Thank you for reading Deadly Sabotage. I hope you enjoyed it. One of my favorite aspects of writing a novel is the research. Sometimes all my research is done from a distance—YouTube, blogs, internet, books and conversations with experts. But other times I get the opportunity to take a research trip, and for this book I visited Mt. St. Helens. The very cool thing about it is that, as of last year, I only live an hour away. I grew up in Texas and I remember watching the news replay the dramatic blast of the side of the mountain, and I never dreamed that I would live so close one day. I'm grateful that I now live in the Pacific Northwest, and I can easily visit places where I love to set my stories. I trust the Lord to guide me regarding any spiritual messages and I especially love that this story is about trading beauty for ashes, and Mt. St. Helens is certainly an amazing backdrop and a perfect example of God's creation and how he turns ash into something beautiful. Remember, God is for you! I love connecting with my readers. You can learn how to connect and find out more about me and my books at ElizabethGoddard.com

Many blessings,
Elizabeth Goddard

Get 3 FREE REWARDS!

We'll send you 2 FREE Books plus a FREE Mystery Gift.

FREE Value Over **$20**

Both the **Harlequin® Special Edition** and **Harlequin® Heartwarming™** series feature compelling novels filled with stories of love and strength where the bonds of friendship, family and community unite.

YES! Please send me 2 FREE novels from the Harlequin Special Edition or Harlequin Heartwarming series and my FREE Gift (gift is worth about $10 retail). After receiving them, if I don't wish to receive any more books, I can return the shipping statement marked "cancel." If I don't cancel, I will receive 6 brand-new Harlequin Special Edition books every month and be billed just $5.49 each in the U.S. or $6.24 each in Canada, a savings of at least 12% off the cover price, or 4 brand-new Harlequin Heartwarming Larger-Print books every month and be billed just $6.24 in the U.S. or $6.74 each in Canada, a savings of at least 19% off the cover price. It's quite a bargain! Shipping and handling is just 50¢ per book in the U.S. and $1.25 per book in Canada.* I understand that accepting the 2 free books and gift places me under no obligation to buy anything. I can always return a shipment and cancel at any time by calling the number below. The free books and gift are mine to keep no matter what I decide.

Choose one:
☐ **Harlequin Special Edition** (235/335 BPA GRMK)
☐ **Harlequin Heartwarming Larger-Print** (161/361 BPA GRMK)
☐ **Or Try Both!** (235/335 & 161/361 BPA GRPZ)

Name (please print)

Address _____ Apt. #

City _____ State/Province _____ Zip/Postal Code

Email: Please check this box ☐ if you would like to receive newsletters and promotional emails from Harlequin Enterprises ULC and its affiliates. You can unsubscribe anytime.

Mail to the **Harlequin Reader Service:**
IN U.S.A.: P.O. Box 1341, Buffalo, NY 14240-8531
IN CANADA: P.O. Box 603, Fort Erie, Ontario L2A 5X3

Want to try 2 free books from another series? Call 1-800-873-8635 or visit www.ReaderService.com.